Tempting the Wild Wolf

RAYNA TYLER

ALSO BY RAYNA TYLER

Seneca Falls Shifters

Tempting the Wild Wolf
Captivated by the Cougar
Enchanting the Bear
Enticing the Wolf
Teasing the Tiger

Ketaurran Warriors

Jardun's Embrace
Khyron's Claim
Zaedon's Kiss
Rygael's Reward
Logan's Allure

Crescent Canyon Shifters

Engaging His Mate
Impressing His Mate

CHAPTER ONE

Mandy

For some reason, walking into the living room of the old cabin felt as if I were entering someone's home uninvited. I strained to listen, to see if I could hear even the slightest noise to confirm that my uneasy feeling wasn't anything more than my active imagination. Even though the only sound that greeted me was the creaking of floorboards under my feet, I wasn't completely reassured.

The Seneca Falls Resort had been closed for business for the last few months, and all the rentals, including this one, were supposed to be unoccupied. Realistically, I knew the building was empty because it was being renovated, and I was one of the people hired to do some of the work.

A musty smell lingered in the air, and, judging by the thin layer of dust on the half wall separating the kitchen from the living room, I'd say the place hadn't seen any decent cleaning in a while. Although there was plenty of light to find my way, I was tempted to open the blinds covering the picture window to let in some of the early morning sunlight and dispel my nervous tension.

Instead, I shrugged off my imaginings, crossed to the

other side of the living room, and headed down the short, narrow hallway leading to the back of the house. Once I'd located the entrance to the small bathroom, I ran my hand along the wall until I found the switch for the overhead light and gave it a flick.

The bathroom had a vanity-style sink and a bathtub that also served as a shower. The almond-colored toilet sitting in the corner appeared out of place compared to the remainder of the room, which was equipped and accessorized in white. It wasn't overly large, and two people could fit in here comfortably with only a minimal amount of elbow rubbing.

I placed my rectangular black-and-yellow toolbox along with the short plastic bucket I'd clasped in one hand on the floor against the only unused wall. Next, I pulled the bundle of dry, clean rags and towels I'd tucked under my other arm and dropped them in the same spot. I liked being prepared and always brought along extras in case any of my jobs got messy. And being a plumber/handyperson meant there were times when messy wasn't an exaggeration.

I examined the dilapidated cabinet that housed the pipes for the bathroom's single sink. Long, thin cracks marred the faux wood finish, and the porcelain inside the bowl had been badly chipped. The destruction was obviously due to human mistreatment and abuse, not the usual wear and tear expected over time.

As in several of the other units I'd visited with Reese Reynolds, one of the new owners of the mountain resort, this one would have to be replaced. The repairs weren't going to fix themselves, so I could either continue to stare at them or get to work. With a resigned sigh, I snagged one of the towels from the stack and stretched it out on the vinyl floor tiling in front of the vanity to protect my bare knees.

The June temperatures usually hit the eighties. None of the cabins had air-conditioning, so I preferred to wear shorts to work. Since I wasn't required to make a fashion statement, my current outfit—one of my favorites—was a blue tank top and some cutoff overalls.

I knelt next to the cabinet and opened the two single-paneled doors to examine what I'd be dealing with. I was glad to see that the original piping had shut-off valves for the cold and hot water. Provided both of the powder-coated valves worked, I wouldn't have to mess with finding the main and turning off the water for the entire building. Definitely a good thing, because I'd have to crawl under the porch to find it.

One problem at a time.

The shelf on the lower part of the cabinet contained a few puddles of water, was badly stained, and parts of the wood showed signs of rotting, another reason the entire unit needed to go. I leaned closer to examine the drainage pipe. It was metal, encrusted with rust, and had at least one thin crack beginning near the edge of the seal.

I shook my head and frowned, then reached inside and unwrapped a moldy old rag from around the pipe, wondering who the idiot was who thought the flimsy piece of fabric would work to fix the leak. Would it have killed them to temporarily patch it with a little duct tape? There's a reason they say it has one hundred and one uses.

The rag was damp, and I was surprised to find moisture on the metal where my hand brushed against it, an indication that someone had recently used the sink. Dread, along with the feeling of not being alone, skittered across my skin. I tried to convince myself it was nothing, that Reese had turned on the water during another one of his inspections.

After a couple of hard cranks, and a few silent prayers that the old metal wouldn't disintegrate in my hands, I was able to turn the valves. Rising on my knees, I twisted the faucet handles to ensure the water was completely turned off. Next, I snagged another towel off the stack and used it to sop up the water on the shelf, then placed my bucket underneath the pipes. After grabbing a wrench out of the toolbox, I lay on my side and angled my upper body inside the cabinet so I could reach the pipes connected to the faucets behind the bowl of the sink.

Of course, banging my head and having a sharp pain blast across my skull was not part of the plan. "Mother of pearl...that hurt," I grumbled and reached for the top of my head. Turning slightly, I glanced behind me and found a tarnished nail, bent at an angle, protruding from the wall. It looked as if someone had trouble pounding it all the way in and had decided to leave it. I glared at the evil piece of metal, thankful I was up-to-date on my tetanus shots.

I'd lost count of how many times over the years I'd banged my head or other parts of my body and ended up bruised, scraped, or bleeding. Clearly, Roy Jenson, my employer and father, had stretched the truth when he'd taught me the skills of the trade and said being a plumber wasn't a hazardous job. I was certain this was his fault, because I refused to believe my propensity for injury had anything to do with my clumsy tendencies. Okay, I'll admit I wasn't the most graceful of people—more like the complete opposite. But I was darned good at my job, and that was all that mattered, right?

At least when I rubbed my fingertips across my scalp, I didn't feel anything wet and sticky, so there was a good chance I hadn't cut myself. Although, if someone shaved my honey-blonde hair, I was pretty sure they'd find a road map attesting to all the times I'd injured my head while working underneath sinks or replacing the plumbing in tight areas.

After more uncomfortable maneuvering and skinning my right elbow on the wall, I finally got the wrench clamped around the section of pipe where I wanted it. Several twists later, I heard a low, deep, threatening growl, and the tingle along my spine was back.

Crap, with a damn thrown in for good measure. Was that a dog? And if it was, how did it get inside? Reese didn't have any pets, and I hadn't seen any dogs running around outside when I'd arrived. I loved animals, especially the furry, domestic variety, but had no interest in becoming a chew toy.

Whatever was growling sounded big, close, and very angry. My muscles tensed, and my heart raced loud enough to make my ears pound. From this position, I couldn't see the doorway, and I wished I could pull my long, exposed legs into the cabinet with me. If it was a dog, it was possible it had been abandoned or belonged to one of Reese's neighbors. No matter how hard I tried, I couldn't stop images of an angry Rottweiler or a snarling German shepherd from slipping into my mind.

I stifled a groan when my imagination decided to toss in an image of a bear. And not just any bear, but a big black one with sharp teeth. Bears were common in the southern Colorado wilderness. Personally, I'd never seen one, but that didn't mean one hadn't wandered onto the grounds and was now planning to make me its lunch. I'll admit there were times when I get distracted and have a bad habit of leaving doors open. I quickly sifted through my memories, trying to remember if I'd at least secured the screen portion of the double door when I'd entered the cabin. Not that a screen was a deterrent for a large predator.

I hated the idea of hurting an animal, but if it came down to thwacking it over the head or me losing a chunk of flesh from my leg, I would choose thwacking. With narrow hips and breasts that lacked the ability to make decent cleavage, I wasn't model material. At twenty-six, this body was all I had, and I planned to keep it long past reaching twenty-seven.

The wrench I clutched tightly in my sweaty hand was the only weapon I had available. Slowly, without making any jerky movements, I slipped it off the pipe and eased myself backward out of the cabinet. I bumped my head on the inside of the wooden frame and bit back the flow of curse words rapidly forming on the tip of my tongue. Threat of death or not, I was honoring my deceased mother's wishes by not using the "F" word, even if it made me feel better and the circumstances warranted a good rant.

I'd barely gotten out of the cabinet when I heard another growl, this one much closer, and I froze. I inhaled deeply, then slowly turned my head so I could get a glimpse of whatever was standing in the doorway. I widened my eyes because what I saw wasn't even close to what I'd expected.

This was not a dog or a bear. There were no paws, no fur, or even four legs. What had me cornered in the bathroom was much worse and far deadlier. And right now, I'd rather be facing one of my first two choices.

Crouched in the doorway was a man. A man with two sharp fangs, and claws extending from his fingertips. Okay, so he wasn't entirely a man. More like a man on the verge of transforming into an animal, a shifter. He glared at me with silvery-gray eyes made more noticeable by the darkening hue rimming his irises. His chest and feet were bare, black sweatpants the only thing covering his lower body.

There had to be something wrong with me. I was scared to the point of peeing my pants and should have been screaming until my lungs hurt. Instead, I stared with appreciation at the way his mussed, shiny black hair touched his shoulders and admiring the smooth tone to his pronounced pectorals and the thick muscles flexing in his arms.

Most of the people living in the nearby town of Ashbury had no idea shifters existed, but I did. Because of my friendship with Berkley, Reese's sister, I'd discovered their existence by accident when she'd saved my life. When James Reynolds, the resort's previous owner, was still alive, Berkley and Reese had spent a few weeks of their summer vacations with their grandfather. I could remember every detail of that horrible day as if the eleven years since then hadn't passed.

Back then, the resort was doing well. It was shortly after my fifteenth birthday and I was camping with some of my girlfriends. I'd somehow gotten separated from the group and came across two older boys who were staying in one of the outlying cabins. They thought it would be fun to show me their wolves, scare the hell out of me, and chase me through the forest before doing who knows what else to me.

Luckily, Berkley had been out on a run and heard my screams. Her wolf tore through the trees, snarling, snapping, and protectively pacing between me and the other wolves. Reese showed up a few minutes later. Even as a teen, he was a much larger, fiercer wolf. One look at him and even I knew who'd win if there was a fight. It didn't take long for the two boys to come to the same conclusion and take off running.

Afterward, Berkley shifted into her human form and walked me back to my campsite. Once the shock wore off, I had lots of questions. Questions she didn't mind answering with the stipulation that I didn't share them with anyone else. The existence of shifters wasn't common knowledge, and I was honored to be trusted with the information.

That day marked the beginning of a close friendship, one I'd cherished for many years and was still ongoing. Since I'd witnessed my friend's transformation on numerous occasions, I was certain the man filling most of the doorway with his large frame was a wolf in a partial shift. He'd allowed enough of his animal to surface in order to frighten what he considered a threat. Me.

I was smart enough to know it was never a good idea to challenge a shifter, even if the change is partial. After setting the wrench on the floor, I kept my gaze focused on his chest and lowered my head in a submissive manner. Not that staring at his chest was a hardship.

Berkley also taught me that during any part of a shift, the animal still maintains their human side and could understand what was being said to them. "Easy there, Fido. I come in peace." Using sarcasm probably wasn't a good choice, but it was my natural defense mechanism in scary situations. It was either that or start screaming. I knew that screaming would make me seem like prey, and, according to Berkley, wolves loved going after prey. It was better to stick with sarcasm. I might live longer.

If I didn't end up as this guy's breakfast, I planned to let Reese know how uncool it was not to tell me ahead of time that the cabin was occupied, or that its new owner was a huge, intimidating wolf.

His responding growl sounded more like a snort and a lot less threatening. I allowed some of the tension to ease from my body and sat back on my haunches.

"Please don't eat me."

This time I got a grunt rather than a snort and felt I was making progress. "There has been some kind of misunderstanding. If you let me use my phone, I'll call someone who can clear this mess up." I glanced at his face and patiently waited for a response.

He narrowed his eyes suspiciously, studying me with a piercing intensity. After a few long and tense moments of silence, he nodded.

Unlike him, I was big on communication and didn't want him to think I was a threat. "I'm going to reach into my pocket and pull out my phone, okay?" After retrieving the cell from my bib pocket, I ran my thumb over one of the speed dial numbers. I wasn't interested in wasting time with pleasantries and blurted out what I needed to say as soon as I heard a familiar male voice on the other end of the call. "Reese, it's Mandy. Please get your ass over to cabin forty-one now. One of your guys has me trapped in the bathroom and looks like he's about to go feral."

"Fuck," was all I heard before the call disconnected.

Satisfied that help was on the way, I slid the phone

back into my pocket and decided to get a better look at the guy while I waited.

Ashbury is a small town. I'd lived there my whole life, knew pretty much everyone, and didn't remember ever seeing him before. I might be forgetful, but I'd have a hard time forgetting someone this good-looking.

I tried not to stare, but it was difficult to keep my eyes from wandering to the smooth, tanned skin covering those serious abs. Even crouching, he was massive, and I calculated his height to be at least six feet when standing. Dark stubble ran along his defined jaw, and I wondered if his hair was as silky as it appeared. I'd bet anything his wolf had a gorgeous fur coat.

"I'm not feral," he muttered. He'd been quiet for so long and his deep voice was so low, I almost didn't hear him.

I stopped drooling over his chest and snapped my gaze back to his face. "I'm sorry, what did you say?"

"I'm not feral." This time, his voice was louder, a deep baritone that sent pleasant flutters through my insides.

Now that he was actually speaking to me, I felt a little braver. "Could have fooled me...what with the whole badass fangs-and-claws thing you have going on." I waved my hand through the air. "Besides, isn't there a rule about showing them off to the locals?" It wasn't a criminal offense or anything, but Berkley had told me there was an unspoken rule that shifters aren't supposed to expose themselves to humans, except on rare occasions. Saving my life had fallen into that category.

A brief glint of hurt flashed across his serious expression as if I'd somehow insulted him with my comments. He flexed his fingers, and the claws magically disappeared, followed a few seconds later by the large fangs. "Better?" His sarcasm mirrored my own.

"Much." Since he'd scared the crap out of me, I was finding it hard to feel bad about hurting his feelings.

"Mandy?" Reese's gruff bellow reached the bathroom

at the same time I heard what sounded like the front door banging loudly against a wall.

"In here," I called, keeping my focus on the stranger.

Reese appeared in the hallway, his chest heaving and a hint of red flushing his cheeks. I wasn't sure if the color was induced by anger or from having to run from the lodge to get here. I was leaning toward irritation since I knew Reese was in good shape. He's a good-looking guy, and I couldn't remember ever seeing an ounce of fat on him. Not that I'd ever spent time perusing or anything.

"Nick, why are you terrorizing my help?" Reese growled at the man getting to his feet.

Nick? Was this the stepbrother Berkley had mentioned, the resort's third partner?

Nick squared his shoulders and faced Reese. He was every bit as tall as Reese, maybe an inch or so taller, and I commended myself on my earlier assessment. Both of them were huge mountains of muscle, contrasting in appearance yet equally attractive in their own way.

Where Nick had the whole dark-hair-and-complexion thing covered, Reese leaned toward the lighter side. His eyes were brown with a hint of amber, and his cropped, chocolate-brown hair was laced with several lighter shades and compared closely to Berkley's.

"Your help"—Nick snarled and pointed in my direction—"was invading my home."

Invading his home? Was he kidding? It wasn't as if I'd brought a rifle and was shooting up the place. Groaning, I grabbed my wrench off the floor and used the counter to stand. I immediately regretted the move when the blood rushed to my legs and a painful tingle shot across my skin.

"You should have checked in." Reese spoke to Nick and pinched the bridge of his nose. "I wasn't expecting you back until next week. Mandy would have been done by then."

"It was late, and I was tired," Nick said.

Even though Nick's comment irritated me, I couldn't

stop staring at him. He fascinated me more than any man I'd ever met, and I hoped I wasn't drooling. They were too busy sharing heated looks and not paying any attention to me, so I assumed I was okay.

I didn't want to be trapped in the bathroom if their argument suddenly got worse. "Excuse me." I waited until I had their full attention before continuing, "If my presence is going to bother Mr. Furball..." Sometimes I held a grudge longer than I should. "I can work on one of the other cabins."

Reese roughly swept his hand along the side of his head. "No, I need the work on this cabin finished first. It's the worst one on the property. Mr. Fur...I mean Nick won't have a problem with it, will you?" The question sounded more like an order, one he emphasized with a daring glare.

Nick was back to scrutinizing me, and the way his gaze roamed over my body had ripples of warmth coursing through me. I had to admit I was disappointed when he finally returned his attention to Reese. "No, no problem." There was a low growl attached to Nick's grumble.

"Good, meet me at the lodge. You can fill me in on your trip." Reese stepped aside to make room for Nick to leave.

"Should I be worried?" I asked Reese once I believed Nick was out of earshot.

"He's fine." Reese didn't sound convincing, and I didn't feel reassured.

"Am I going to have problems with the rest of the cabins?" I didn't want any more surprises. I was under the impression the cabins were for paying guests and wondered why Nick wasn't staying at the lodge with his brother and sister.

"The rest of them are unoccupied. Nick likes his space, which is why..." Reese sighed, answering my unspoken question. "Just let me know if you need anything else, okay?"

"Sure." I understood the need for personal space but got the impression by Reese's frown that there was more about Nick's situation that he wasn't telling me. If I wasn't being paid well and didn't desperately need the money to help pay the ever-growing stack of doctor bills my father had accumulated after his leg injury, I'd be tempted to tell Reese what he could do with his job.

As soon as I heard the front door shut behind Reese, I sagged against the counter. Putting up with a territorial wolf was *not* what I'd signed up for when I'd agreed to do this project. Even if said wolf was gorgeous and I was attracted to his territorial bad-boy persona in the worst way.

CHAPTER TWO

NICK

After leaving the bathroom, I headed to the bedroom and slipped out of my sweats and into a pair of jeans. I'd been hard from the minute I'd inhaled Mandy's scent—a combination of woman and wildflowers. If she was going to be in my home for a few days, wearing constricting pants would be easier to disguise any further erections.

I grabbed the old T-shirt I'd tossed on the chair the night before, then slipped on my boots and exited the cabin. Going barefoot through the woods didn't bother me, but because Reese had humans working on the property and at the lodge, I needed to appear somewhat presentable. Most of the employees weren't aware that my siblings and I could shift into wolves.

I could go back to being comfortable once I returned to the privacy of my cabin. Actually, I'd prefer not to leave the cabin at all. Mandy and her intoxicating scent were the reason I wanted to stay. If I wasn't mistaken, I'd also smelled the sweet hint of strawberry, something she used to bathe with or wash her hair. I bit back a groan and imagined her naked with water cascading across her skin.

Thinking about her made me hard again and had my

wolf prancing and ready to beg for any attention she'd be willing to give us. I needed to push her from my mind and focus my thoughts on the meeting with Reese.

It had been nearing midnight by the time I'd gotten back from my trip to Denver. I'd spent most of my life avoiding the bigger cities. Even when I lived in small towns, getting a full night of rest without worry was something I'd rarely experienced. Out here, the stress-free location coupled with the fresh mountain air lulled me into a deep sleep.

Normally, I'd awaken at the slightest noise. I hadn't heard Mandy enter my home and was groggy when I'd heard noises coming from the bathroom. Years of practiced control was the only thing that kept me from fully shifting. By the time I realized my wolf was partially out, I was crouched in the doorway and she'd seen me.

At the first flash of claws, most humans would be screaming, but not Mandy. Sure, I'd scented her initial fear—a reaction to my growling—and knew I'd scared her. Instead of cowering in a corner, she'd responded with sarcasm and respectfully acknowledged the dominance of my wolf.

I smiled, remembering Mandy's humor and the way she'd handled the situation. Other than Berkley, no other female had ever dared to show courage when faced with the threat of my wolf.

Mate. My wolf pushed the word into my mind. No, that couldn't be right, I argued. What were the odds of finding the one woman specifically meant for me? And in my bathroom no less.

Not good to impossible since I didn't have that kind of luck. My wolf disagreed. The contrary animal didn't care about luck. He snarled at me, convinced the female with the luscious long legs and one of the finest asses I'd ever seen was our mate.

I paused to breathe in the fresh air and scent of pine. I fought the urge to return to the cabin and kick my brother out so I could explore my supposed connection to Mandy. Rather than test the boundaries of our newly formed relationship, I followed Reese's instruction and hiked the worn path that weaved between the tall ash trees and to the back entrance of the main lodge.

Out of all the buildings on the property, this one received the most maintenance and required only a minimal amount of work before it would be fully functional. The lodge had two levels, the lower containing a lobby, offices, and a restaurant. The upper floor was comprised of rooms for guests who preferred to stay at the lodge rather than rent one of the pricier cabins.

The outside had a slanted, shingled roof, and the exterior walls were crafted with sawed logs stacked horizontally and stained with a light wood finish. The interior walls had a similar construction. There were ornate support beams evenly spaced at ceiling level throughout all the open areas. The main entrance area had a huge fireplace and hearth with a slate-rock finish.

Opposite the offices and segregated from the guest portion of the building was an additional wing explicitly designed for the owners and any staff who might need to stay the night if the weather got too bad for traveling. That section had five bedrooms, two of which were occupied by Reese and Berkley. I'd turned down their offer to take one of the three remaining rooms. With the temperament and nature of my wolf, I'd learned a solitary home away from other people was usually best.

Up until three months ago, when Berkley found me, I'd thought I was an only child and wasn't aware I had any siblings. My mother, gone for twelve years now, led me to believe my father had died shortly after I'd been born. Truth was—according to my new half sister—the sorry son of a bitch had refused to acknowledge my existence and was alive and well with a new family somewhere on the East Coast. He'd also walked out on Berkley and Reese when they were teenagers.

Apparently, the man didn't believe in waiting for his true mate to start a family. He had a history of discarding one female for another and hadn't wanted to be bothered by his children.

I still wasn't sure how Berkley had convinced me to move to the isolated mountain resort. Actually, that wasn't true. I had my reasons for avoiding humans, people in general, and living in a secluded area was a big draw. The relationship between the three of us was tenuous at best, but I'd discovered Berkley could be very persuasive when she wanted something. Right now, she was determined to keep us together and turn us into a family. Something I'd never truly had, had tended to avoid, yet secretly yearned for.

After entering the building, I strolled down the hall and into the largest of three offices. I was too keyed up to sit while I waited, so I walked over to the double-paned window and stared at the panoramic view outside. My thoughts returned to Mandy and the way I'd overreacted.

Old habits caused by years of painful memories are hard to break. I knew I should have backed off as soon as I'd realized she wasn't a threat. My wolf was curious, and it took everything I had to keep the damned thing from completing the shift. Not because my animal wanted to hurt her, but because he was intrigued by her scent. *Mate*, my wolf whispered again.

I ignored him. To argue with him was a wasted effort because he wasn't an ordinary wolf. He was part wild wolf and prone to be more aggressive and short-tempered. It was a known fact that wild wolves didn't survive well around other shifters, and humans even less. It was why our kind avoided heavily populated areas as much as possible.

The full-blooded ones, including some of my distant relatives, lived like gypsies, always moving, never settling down. A lot of them took odd jobs to survive. Thinking about my lineage reminded me of my mother, a loss that pained me. Faulty machinery at the small traveling carnival where we worked had taken her life when I was sixteen. Shortly afterward, I'd run away. There was no way I was going to let the sleazy owner force me to shift so he could lock me in a cage and put me on display for his customers.

I'd spent the last twelve years taking one job after another, staying in each place only long enough to make some money before moving on to the next. I'd never gotten involved with any females for more than a few weeks. I'd never made any lasting commitments, always took care of myself, and never looked back. I'd never had a place I wanted to call home.

Until now.

I'd promised Berkley I'd give the family thing a year. A promise I was determined to keep no matter how difficult or uncomfortable staying in one place made me feel. As far as I was concerned, a man who didn't honor his word wasn't much of a man.

I didn't have long to wait before my enhanced hearing detected Reese's familiar stride padding along the wooden floors in the outside hall. Though I was equally as strong and more dominant than my half brother, the wild side of my wolf recognized and respected his leadership. I sensed his power and the agitation radiating from his wolf the moment he entered the room.

Reese propped his ass on the surface of the wooden desk rather than take a seat in the worn leather chair. It was something he did frequently when he was attempting to put someone at ease. He dangled his right leg over the edge, the toe of his boot grazing the hardwood floor.

I preferred to remain standing and braced for the lecture I knew was coming. Unlike me, Reese is usually calm and rarely loses his temper. His demeanor is no doubt a result of the disciplined training he'd received during his four years in the military. I'd noticed on more than one occasion how he studied a situation, object, or opponent, then carefully chose his words before speaking—similar to what he was doing now.

Reese clasped his hands together on his thigh. "I know we've discussed this before, but I want to make sure you understand that not all the humans working on site will be aware of our kind. Some will be helping with the renovations and others will be hired for staff once the place is up and running."

Even though I understood Reese's concerns, it irritated me that he assumed I needed the reminder. I swallowed my growl and gave him the reassurance I knew he was searching for. "I'm aware, and it won't be a problem."

Full wild wolves tended to go feral when provoked. It was another reason they avoided living in areas heavily populated by humans. I'd come close to going feral a few times, but could honestly say I'd never lost control of my wolf.

"Mandy's going to be working in your cabin for the next few days, then moving on to the rest. I've known her and her father for years and trust both of them." Reese tapped the desk reflectively. "I need to know she will be safe, that you're not going to do anything else to upset her."

I had no interest in explaining my actions. I wasn't comfortable telling Reese how after I'd woken and scented Mandy, I'd been overwhelmed by the instinct to claim, not kill. A first for me. Until I could confirm one way or another whether my wolf's suspicions were accurate, I planned to remain silent on the topic.

Reese had taken the lead role in this operation, and I didn't blame him for being frustrated. I needed to keep him pacified so he wouldn't ask me to stay away from her completely. Not that it would matter since my wolf and I weren't good at following orders. I would, however, prefer not to be at odds with my brother. "I won't hurt her, if that's what you're insinuating."

Reese scratched the back of his head. "I'm not insinuating anything, and I wasn't worried about her safety around you. Not only is she good, but she's the only available plumber in Ashbury. We can't afford for her to quit, not with all the other problems we've been having."

By problems, I knew he meant the break-ins and damage being done to some of the outlying cabins. It was the reason we'd hired a local bear shifter for the position of security guard. Although we had no way to prove it, we had a pretty good idea Desmond Bishop, the owner of the Hanover Regency, the expensive hotel on the property adjacent to ours, was behind the vandalism.

Bishop had made it clear via numerous offers that he wanted the resort, or rather the land it sat on, and was determined to own it. We also suspected he was responsible for the problems we'd been having with some of the local suppliers in Hanford, another city in the area. Reese recently tried to purchase some lumber and was turned away. The representative didn't give him any specifics other than to say he was getting pressure from an influential source to refrain from doing business with us.

After receiving the same type of response from other vendors, I'd volunteered for the trip to Denver. I might not have many friends, but I did have connections with people from my time spent working in construction. One of those associates worked in the city, and after some casual drinking and heavy negotiating, he was willing to help us get the supplies we needed.

"I'll be on my best behavior." I tried to sound as convincing as possible.

Reese forced a smile, and it was the first time I'd notice the darkened circles beneath his eyes. I immediately felt guilty for the additional stress I'd caused him and for contemplating telling him to shove it. Truth was I had nowhere else to go. My old life wasn't anything to rave about. The least I could do after everything my siblings had done for me was to give them my support.

Reese raised one brow and didn't appear to be totally convinced, so for good measure, I threw in, "I promise."

He grinned, shrugging some of the rigidness from his shoulders. "Thanks, I appreciate it."

CHAPTER THREE

MANDY

The late-morning sun had been pounding down on this side of the cabin for the last few hours, and the warmth inside the small bathroom was almost unbearable. I raised the dusty blind covering the rectangular window above the toilet. A few grunts and groans later, I had the lower panel lifted enough to allow some fresh air in through the outer screen.

The resort held a lot of good memories for me. Most of them involved the time during my teenage years that I'd spent with Berkley. And, on the rare occasion, with Reese when he wasn't being a macho jerk. As with most maturing males, he'd been too busy trying to impress the local girls and didn't want to be saddled with his younger sister.

I blew out a heavy sigh, realizing four years had passed since I'd spent any quality time on the property or visited the lodge. The summer before Berkley started college was the last time I remembered seeing James Reynolds. What happened to the old man was a tragedy, and more than once, I'd regretted not making the time to come out and visit him.

I stared out the window at the hill in the distance. Slivers of the main lodge peeked through the varying shades of green on the thick wall of trees behind the cabin. Not for the first time, images of Nick and his intense silver-gray eyes popped into my mind. I chastised myself for lingering and hoping I'd catch a glimpse of him returning.

Reese, Berkley, and Nick, the brother I didn't know existed until recently, inherited the run-down resort from their grandfather. There were ten cabins on the property. During my tour with Reese to document the much-needed repairs, he'd mentioned their plans to build more units if the resort did as well as they hoped. He also told me he didn't trust anyone else to do the work, which was why he'd hired Jenson Plumbing.

After my father broke his leg and damaged his ankle, his physician had ordered him to refrain from any type of exertion—what Roy Jenson considered house arrest—the workload was assigned to my capable hands.

I might have learned a lot about being a handyperson from my father, but my real passion, my life's dream, was getting a degree for interior decorating and someday having my own business. I was halfway through the first semester of online courses when I'd had to quit to take care of my father. Plumbing jobs occurred at all hours and there simply wasn't enough time during the day for me to maintain a full-time job and have the time left over to apply to my studies.

Putting my dream on hold to work at the resort wasn't my first choice, but hey, the pay was good, and it helped with the large stack of medical bills. My father was a proud man and didn't want my help, but being the stubborn and loving daughter that I am, I didn't give him a choice.

I turned away from the window and forced myself to get back to work. As far as projects went, the repairs needed in most of the cabins weren't bad, not like some of the other older properties in the area. I'd helped my father on a couple of jobs where the majority of the plumbing was outdated and so bad, it had to be replaced.

Unfortunately, Nick's home was the worst, and I figured it would take me at least another day or so to complete the job. And that was only if I had all the parts I needed.

My stomach rumbled, reminding me that I'd been in a hurry this morning and hadn't taken the time to grab something to eat. Glancing at my watch, I noticed it was almost eleven and decided it was a good time to stop and eat my lunch. Since I couldn't use the water in the bathroom, I headed to the kitchen to wash my hands.

I went out to the truck and dug a bottled water and a sealed plastic bag containing my sliced ham and cheese sandwich out of my favorite cooler. The scrapes and gouges on its dull maroon exterior were a testament to the container's endurance and the many jobs I'd taken it on.

My mind kept drifting back to Nick. Other than a few tidbits Berkley had shared with me, I didn't know much about him, and I had to admit I was curious. It wasn't the stalker type of curious where I was willing to go through his drawers or anything. It was the he-is-a-hot-guy kind of curious, and for the first time in a long time, I was intrigued. Sometimes you could learn a lot about a person simply by seeing how they lived. After quickly eating my sandwich, I decided to check out the rest of his home.

I unscrewed the cap on my water and took a swig as I walked into the living room. I left the main door open so I could see more of the room and take some time to appreciate the rustic appearance. All the walls had long horizontal strips of wood, stained and sealed with a natural finish. The surface was bare, no pictures or artwork to give me any clues about Nick's personality. Either he hadn't had a chance to settle in yet, or he wasn't big on decorating.

There was a blue plaid couch and chair with worn

cushions. Based on the amount of dust on each, I'd bet they were left over from when James ran the resort. Sitting in the middle of the room was a square wooden coffee table. It appeared to be newly handcrafted, not one purchased from a store. The natural tone was beautiful, and I couldn't resist kneeling on the hardwood floor next to it and running my hand admiringly along the wood. The finish was smooth, not a flaw anywhere along the surface.

Surprisingly, I couldn't wield a hammer or do anything carpentry-wise no matter how hard I tried, and I was envious of the skilled person who'd obviously put a lot of time and care into building the exquisite piece. "Very impressive," I said out loud as I ran my fingertips along the ornate designs carved into the wooden legs.

"I'm glad you like it."

I startled at the male voice coming from behind me and jumped to my feet, almost dropping the half-full bottle in my hand. I spun around and found Nick leaning against the doorframe with his arms crossed and an amused grin on his face.

Damn sneaky shifter. He'd been so quiet, I hadn't heard him open the screen door. "Don't do that." I pressed my hand against my chest and could feel the vibration from my poor racing heart.

"You mean enter my own home?"

He had me there. Technically, I had permission to be in the cabin, but from his perspective—one he'd already pointed out—I was an intruder. It didn't, however, give him the right to stand there and act all smug about it or keep scaring the crap out of me.

He raised a challenging brow, then walked into the room, each step a fluid movement reminding me I was dealing with a predator. He didn't stop until he stood two feet away from me. Close enough for me to get a whiff of his male scent, a delightful mixture of musk and the forest. So irresistible that I had to restrain myself from leaning closer.

He wore jeans, not the sweats I'd seen him in earlier. Though he'd covered his chest with a T-shirt, it wasn't hard to see the well-defined muscles through the thin fabric. I grasped my water bottle with both hands, fighting the temptation to examine his chest the same way I had the table.

After what had happened with Craig last year, I'd been adamant about avoiding men. I'd even reached the point where a handsome man's smile didn't affect me. So why did this complete stranger unsettle me in the most delicious, panty-wetting way?

I forced my gaze to meet his unnerving stare. It was as if he was studying me, reaching deep inside my soul and absorbing every part of my being. I'd never experienced anything like it and took a nervous step backward. I searched my muddled mind for a safe topic to distract him and latched on to the table. "Did you make this?" For something to do, I leaned forward and ran my hand over the smooth surface again.

"Yes."

"It's really beautiful."

"I agree."

I thought he was being arrogant and glanced over my shoulder, prepared to make a sarcastic comment, then realized he was looking at me and not the table. I could feel the heat rising on my cheeks. At this rate, red was going to be my natural color. "Okay, then. I should get back to work and let you do…whatever it is you need to do." I didn't wait for a response, moving quickly to get through the door. Once outside, I didn't stop moving until I'd reached the company truck and was leaning my back against the sun-kissed metal.

I took a few deep breaths and stared at the closed screen door, wondering how long it was going to take me to conjure up the nerve to go back inside and finish my work.

NICK

When I'd returned to my cabin and found Mandy lovingly caressing the product of my craftsmanship, I was instantly hard and wondered what it would be like to have those small hands doing the same thing to my body. I could tell by the arousal in her scent, the reddened flush on her skin, and the way her crystalline blue gaze darkened that she was attracted to me as well.

So why had she rushed from the room? Confused and disappointed by Mandy's sudden departure, I walked over to the window in the living room and peeked through the blinds so I could watch her. She rushed down the steps and crossed the gravel drive to the old white truck with Jenson Plumbing emblazoned along the side in big black letters and drop shadowed in yellow.

I knew what to expect from a shifter female; human females, not so much. I hadn't exposed my fangs or claws again, didn't do anything I considered upsetting, so what had I done wrong?

I memorized her features. Even though she did manual labor for a living, her skin appeared soft, and she had a creamy pale complexion. She'd pulled her golden hair into a long braid that reached the middle of her back. I could see a dark blue tank top underneath the overalls that had been fashioned into shorts. They clung tightly to her nice ass and exposed a pair of finely shaped legs. What amused me most were the black socks and ankle-high work boots she'd chosen to complete the ensemble.

I remained there a few minutes longer, internally arguing with my wolf's demands that I go after her. *Mate, mate, mate*, the animal chanted and pranced. I still wasn't convinced, or maybe I was denying our connection because I knew Mandy had been right when she'd accused me of being feral. I was antisocial, a loner, and not fit to be around humans, specifically not someone like her.

I'd never met Mandy before today or associated her with the plumbing company Reese had hired. On the few occasions Berkley had mentioned her friend's name, she'd always spoken very highly of her. After our brief encounter, I'd have to agree with my sister. I could tell Mandy was special and deserved someone better than me, someone who didn't have wild-wolf commitment issues.

I groaned and headed for the kitchen, hoping—no, praying—she returned to the cabin. Otherwise, Reese was going to kill me. Not that I was afraid of my brother. It was easier to use him as an excuse than admit to myself that I selfishly wanted her to come back inside.

I opened the refrigerator and stared at the only two items sitting on the bare shelves: a leftover Styrofoam container and an apple. Whatever was in the container had spoiled. I tossed it in the garbage and reached for the apple. I hadn't bothered to do any stocking before I'd left for the city and needed to do some shopping soon.

I supposed if I got hungry enough, I could always venture into town and dine at one of the only two restaurants. It was either that or eat at the lodge with Berkley and Reese. Although I wouldn't admit it to my siblings, I enjoyed Berkley's cooking and the chance to spend some time with them. The loner part of me craved independence, so I was still figuring out how to compromise with the part of me that longed to be closer to my family.

I leaned against the counter, ready to take a bite out of the apple, when I heard the hinges on the screen squeak. I took a few steps out of the kitchen and saw Mandy standing in the doorway, a handcart loaded with boxes sitting on the porch behind her.

"Do you mind if I"—she pointed toward the bathroom—"finish my work?"

I ignored the anxious knot forming in my stomach. I didn't care what she did—curl up on the couch, join me in bed, anything—as long as she didn't leave. "No, not at all.

Make yourself at home," I said, battling to keep the enthusiasm out of my voice.

She gave me a brief smile, then turned and placed her hand on the tall stack of boxes before tipping the cart toward her. It was bulky and appeared as if she might have trouble getting it inside. Judging by the pictures and descriptions pasted on the side of each cardboard box, I assumed they contained the new cabinet, sink, and faucets for my bathroom.

"Let me help you with that." I placed the apple on the counter and rushed to her side.

Mandy smiled and yanked on the metal bar. "I'm good. I do this all the time." There was a determined set to her jaw.

I didn't want to do anything to upset her or drive her off again, so I stepped aside. I patiently watched her struggle, first with the box on the bottom of her stack when it got hooked on the exterior wall, then when she tried to maneuver the cart's wheels over the base in the doorframe.

Finally, when she released an exasperated groan, I took pity on her and gripped the handle with one hand and eased the cart inside.

"Thanks." She might have been appreciative, but the tone in her voice suggested she was irritated with herself for needing my help.

"No problem. If there's anything else I can help with, let me know." I was standing close and couldn't resist taking another sniff of her tantalizing scent before moving out of the way so she could turn the cart and push it in front of her.

"I'm hoping it won't take more than an hour or so before I'm finished for today, then the bathroom is all yours."

"Take your time. There's no rush." With Mandy in the house, going back to bed to catch up on sleep was not going to happen. Since I couldn't take a shower and my wolf was too interested in staying close to her to go for a run, I was left with nothing to do but hang out and watch her.

I grabbed the apple off the counter and took a bite, unable to stop staring at her luscious ass or the way her long honey-blonde braid swished back and forth as she walked. I moved to the end of the hallway and watched her unload the stack near the bathroom. She pressed the boxes flush against the wall before setting the cart off to the side. I was curious to see what she was doing in the bathroom and couldn't resist following her.

MANDY

Of all the days for me to have problems with my handcart, it had to be today. I didn't usually battle with the metal contraption, much, but with Nick standing so close, I was having trouble thinking, let alone functioning properly. Though he hadn't wolfed out again since our first encounter, I still didn't believe he was thrilled to have me in his home. After watching my incompetence with the cart, I was worried he'd insist Reese find someone else to do my work.

I grabbed the two smaller boxes off the stack, intent on reaching the new vanity on the bottom. I would have to replace the cabinet first before I tackled the new sink and faucets. After setting them off to the side, I turned and came face-to-face with Nick. I was already self-conscious enough without having to endure his close scrutiny. "You aren't going to stand there and watch me work, are you?"

"Maybe." He shrugged and took a bite of his apple.

Breathe, I needed to breathe.

I stood in front of the large cardboard box and worked the edge of the tape securing the lid with my fingernail. Normally, I'd use my utility knife to cut through the plastic seal. With Nick watching my every move, I was afraid I'd end up cutting myself or slicing the contents inside.

After ripping off the tape and lifting the flaps, I lowered the box on its side.

"Why don't you tear the box open to get it out?" Nick was standing so close, I could feel the heat radiating from him.

I glanced at him over my shoulder. "I like to hang on to the box in case I ordered the wrong size and need to return it."

"Makes sense," Nick said before disappearing into the kitchen. He returned a few seconds later without the remnants of his apple.

I ignored my nervousness at having him standing close behind me, then crouched in front of the box, and reached inside, gripping the wooden frame. I tugged, irritated when the protective walls of Styrofoam encasing the cabinet wouldn't budge. When I gripped it from a different angle and pulled harder, my hand slipped. I reeled backward, bumping into Nick and knocking him down, with me on his lap.

"I'm so sorry." I squirmed to get up but couldn't move because his arm was wrapped around my waist.

Feeling his hard shaft pressed firmly against my backside caused an immediate reaction between my legs. It was all I could do not to moan and wonder how much nicer it would feel if I was facing the other direction.

It was nice to know the attraction was mutual. I was certain letting my thoughts continue down this path was a major mistake, one I was determined not to make.

After what happened with Craig and my determination to avoid men, Berkley would be ecstatic that I was entertaining thoughts of having sex again. I wasn't, however, convinced my friend would be glad to hear it was with her newly found brother.

"No harm done." He gripped my hips and lifted until I was standing again.

"I'm not normally such a klutz." Well, I was, but he

didn't need to know that unflattering detail about me.

"How about letting me help?" He grinned and reached for the box. "Unless you'd liked to end up on my lap again."

I laughed at his infectious humor. "I'm okay, thanks." I stepped out of the way.

He effortlessly slid the cabinet, Styrofoam and all, out of its cardboard shell. "Now what?"

"Now we…" I removed the top protective layer to reveal a large ding in the wooden surface. After all that, it would need to be returned and a new one ordered. "…put it back in the box."

CHAPTER FOUR

NICK

Since arriving in Ashbury, I'd gotten into a regular routine of eating one or two meals during the week with my siblings at the lodge. Once the resort was fully operational, Reese planned to hire several cooks and a full staff for the restaurant. Berkley was in charge of developing the menu and enjoyed preparing all the meals. Of course, she had designated Reese and me as her personal taste testers and insisted we make an appearance.

I'd learned to stay out of the way when Berkley was in the kitchen and was waiting in the main room near the lobby for her to let me know it was time to eat. The lodge was located higher up on the hill than the cabins and provided a great view of the mountainside and the rest of the resort. There were several large picture windows on one of the walls, and from here, I could see most of the cabins, at least the ones not enshrouded by tall aspens. I caught intermittent glimpses of Mandy's truck weaving through the trees on her descent back to the highway leading into town.

I couldn't get her tantalizing scent or the way she'd felt

in my arms when I caught her in the hallway out of my mind. I still wasn't sure I believed my wolf's claim that Mandy was our mate. Not that it mattered—I was a loner, broken on so many levels, and she deserved better. An old and familiar panic settled over me. What had I been thinking when I'd told Berkley I'd stay? If I was smart, I'd pack up my few belongings and leave.

"What are you thinking so hard about?" Berkley walked up behind me. She tucked her arm through mine, then leaned her head against my shoulder.

"Nothing much." I continued to watch Mandy's truck and realized Berkley was gazing in the same direction. My sister is exceptionally good at reading people, and I was afraid if I glanced in her direction, she'd be able to tell what I was thinking.

"How are things going with Mandy?"

I turned to face my sister. "What... Nothing happened." The defensive reply was out before I could stop myself.

"I meant with the plumbing." She raised her brow and grinned, confirmation that my response had given her something to ponder. "Reese told me she's working in your cabin first."

"Oh yeah. Fine. She's doing fine." I couldn't believe I was stammering like a teenager who'd been caught making out in the back of his parents' car.

"So, what's with the frown? Want to tell me what's bothering you? You aren't thinking about leaving, are you?"

"Possibly." Any topic, including myself, was preferable to my sister's continued discussion about Mandy. They were close friends, and I wasn't sure how my sister would feel if she found out Mandy might be my mate. *Is our mate*, my wolf snarled.

"You're doing that thing again, aren't you?" She glared, moving to stand in front of me.

"What thing?" I tried to feign innocence, hoping it

would work, yet not surprised when it didn't. Berkley had the determination of an entire pack of wolves when she wanted something.

She propped her hands on her hips. "The *thing* where you think because we grew up differently, you don't have a right to be here, that you don't deserve to have a home like everybody else."

"Maybe." It was uncanny how one knowing look from her could make me—a grown and older male—squirm.

"Well, stop it. You know it doesn't matter to Reese and me if we had different mothers. You're still our brother, and we don't want you to leave."

"But I've been here off and on for almost a month and…" And I was getting comfortable, a completely new experience, and one that scared the hell out of me.

"No buts." Berkley huffed. "This is your home, and I'm holding you to your promise. You have to stay and give it a try. One month is not trying, it's barely getting your paws wet." She snickered at her own humor.

"What about my wolf? What if I…" Lose control. It was something I struggled with regularly and the main reason I avoided humans and never settled down in one place.

"You won't." She patted my arm reassuringly. "You spent all day with Mandy. She's human, and since I spoke with her before she left, I know for a fact that you didn't hurt her."

"That's different. She's…" My mate. I bit back the words, unsettled by how comfortable I was getting with the idea and not willing to share my suspicions with my sister.

"She's what?"

"Nothing." I could feel myself getting in deeper and glanced away from her prying gaze. "You and Reese don't need me around to run the resort."

"Nice try." Berkley playfully punched me in the arm. "You know us better than that. Even without the terms of the will, we want you to stay. You're family and not allowed to run."

Our grandfather, a man I'd never met but who knew all about me, had made me a partial owner of the resort. The document clearly outlined stipulations requiring all three of us to remain together. I knew Berkley couldn't care less about the legal specifications. She was more interested in developing a close relationship with her newly acquired family—mainly me.

"Besides, it would be a waste of time. You know I'll track you down again and drag you back here, so save us both the trouble and say you'll stay.

Of course she would, the tenacious little wolf.

She transformed her grin into a pout. "You're my brother, and it would break my heart if you left."

I could handle a lot of things, having my sister slap me with guilt wasn't one of them. "You win, so stop already." I was a foot taller than her, and it was easy for me to wrap my arm around her neck, pull her close, and ruffle her hair.

"Hey, don't make me hurt you." Berkley giggled, then snagged me into a quick hug before pulling away. "Speaking of quality time, why don't you come with me to the bar tonight?"

"Where did you get quality time from me talking about leaving?" I was confused by her complete change of topic, something she did frequently.

Berkley waved her hand in front of my face as if she couldn't figure out why I didn't get it. "Simple. You're *not* leaving. You *are* family, and family spends time doing fun things together."

Suddenly suspicious, I asked, "How is going to a bar having fun?"

"It's a good way to relieve stress and meet some of the locals."

"Nah, I'm pretty sure I have a bunch of things I'd rather be doing here." I crossed my arms and gave her a stern look.

"Like what, change into your wolf and chase squirrels into trees?"

"Very funny, smart-ass." I reached for her again, but this time, she jumped back and dodged my grasp.

"I guess Mandy and I will have a good time without you." She shrugged innocently.

"Mandy's going?"

"Of course. It's a girls' night out, and you know what that means."

It meant I wasn't going to like the answer. "No, what?"

"It means dancing with a lot of hot guys." Berkley shook her ass to mimic a dance move.

I was right, it wasn't something I wanted to hear. Before I had a chance to offer any objections, Berkley was strutting toward the doorway leading to the restaurant's dining area. "I need to go check on dinner. Let me know if you change your mind." She winked at me over her shoulder, then disappeared from the room.

Mandy going out looking for guys with his sister spelled all kinds of trouble. The kind of trouble that would get a male killed if they even thought about going near her.

Mine. The growl was out before I could stop it. The thought of another man, any man, touching Mandy had my wolf prancing and sent me trailing after my sister to let her know I'd changed my mind and was going to show up at the bar.

CHAPTER FIVE

MANDY

"I'll only be gone for a few hours. Are you sure you'll be all right?" Ever since my father injured his leg, I'd hated to be away from him for too long. Call me overprotective, but the thought of coming home and finding him hurt again made me shudder.

Our home had two stories, and somehow he'd tripped and fallen down part of the staircase. I was the one to find him and still considered it a miracle he hadn't broken his neck. Before the accident, he'd convinced me to temporarily give up my apartment and move back home to save money while I finished school.

With the resort scheduled to open in a few months and having to deal with our company's regular customers, I'd been putting in some long hours. I'd done my best to check in with him once or twice a day and made sure I was home every night.

Thank goodness for Barb, the retired widow who lived next door. She'd been great about keeping an eye on my father. She was the sweetest person ever, but get out of line and she turned into a military drill sergeant. It was exactly what my father needed to make sure he followed the doctor's orders and stayed out of trouble.

The way Barb doted on him made me wonder if she secretly had a crush on him. My mother had been gone a long time now, and I would have loved to see my father find someone special.

I couldn't remember the last time I'd gone out to have some fun—certainly not since Craig—and I was looking forward to spending some time with Berkley. One night where I could let loose and not focus on the past or all the things currently stressing me.

"I'm fine. You know the doc says I'll be able to go back to work soon, so stop worrying about me."

Like the not worrying was going to happen anytime soon. "We'll see." I'd come too close to losing him and wasn't taking any chances.

"Go, have some fun. I can always call Barb if I have any problems." He wiggled his brows, and there was a mischievous glint in his eyes making me wonder if maybe the crush went both ways. "You need to get out more. Find a nice guy, go out on a date, hook up or whatever they're calling it now."

I widened my eyes, and my mouth hung open. I couldn't believe my father, the man who'd threatened to shoot any of my teenage suitors with his shotgun, was insinuating that I should get laid. "Dad, there will be no hooking up or anything else." Well, maybe for Berkley since she didn't have a problem going home with strangers. I, on the other hand, wasn't having casual sex no matter how much my friend insisted a one-night stand would be good for me.

I was a great fan of sex, just not with a stranger. I preferred spending time with a guy and getting to know him before I jumped into bed with him. Though if I ever decided to make an exception to my rule, I would consider Nick. My mind filled with images of his intense silver-gray eyes, and I trembled, remembering how his strong hands felt when he'd held me.

"I want you to know if there is…if you do, I'm fine with it." He cupped my cheeks with both hands and kissed my forehead. He gave me a reassuring smile laced with a flicker of pity. I knew my father too well and realized he was remembering what happened with Craig. Why wouldn't he? He'd been there to witness the worst and most humiliating day of my life. One I'd spent the last year trying to forget.

***

"You ready to have some fun?" Berkley's enthusiastic voice rang through the interior of her car. She was more than ready to have a good time, and it showed. She was decked out like a New York fashion model in a black spaghetti-strap top and slim-fitting pants that tapered at her ankles. Add in the matching heels that I couldn't walk straight in on a good day, and my friend was dressed to kill. I wasn't ready to "strut my stuff," so to speak, and had worn a sleeveless blue blouse, jeans, and a comfortable pair of slip-ons.

"Sure," I answered, filled with trepidation and not sure if I meant it. Even though our relationship had been long-distance for years, friends didn't get any better than Berkley. She knew about Craig, and during the time we both referred to as "the incident," had been away at college working on her marketing degree. I'd turned her down when she offered her support and had wanted to come to Ashbury and stay with me for a few days.

She'd even teased about ripping Craig's balls off for me. Berkley might have insinuated that she was kidding, but I had a feeling she was serious and refused to let her miss school to help me deal with my love life.

She pulled her keys out of the ignition. "Great, then let's go."

She exited the vehicle, and I did the same, closing the

door, then nervously staring at the intimidating wooden building. The Suds 'n' Springs was an average country-style bar complete with an old-fashioned neon sign designed with gold lettering. As far as entertainment went, it was the nearest place within five miles of Ashbury unless you wanted to drive all the way to Hanford, which I didn't. The likelihood of running into Craig was greater, and I was still feeling a little guilty about leaving my father alone. I wanted to be close in case something happened and he needed me.

The lot was already three-quarters full, and several couples were linked hand in hand and headed for the entrance. As soon as they opened the door, the low drone of music and bass filtered outside. For some reason, my feet wouldn't move, and I contemplated whether to let Berkley drag me inside.

Coming here on Friday nights with Craig after our dinner dates had been a regular thing. Something I hadn't attempted since I'd broken things off with him. He'd been the one to cheat on me, and I hadn't wanted to deal with the memories or the sympathetic glances from the people we used to hang out with.

I'd been a tomboy growing up and had a small circle of local female friends. A couple of them had moved away, and the rest were either planning their weddings, raising families, or currently in relationships.

I'd grown tired of hearing how I should get back out there and find another guy. Having my heart ripped out once was plenty. After I'd refused numerous invitations to go out with the girls or be set up on dates, my friends finally stopped asking.

Berkley, on the other hand, wasn't one to take no for an answer. She was convinced all I needed was a great night of sex—no names, no strings—and she was determined to make sure I got it.

Before I had a chance to change my mind, Berkley had me by the arm and was dragging me inside. The place was already packed, not surprising for a Friday night in a town with one movie theater and two restaurants.

"Over there." Berkley pointed at two stools next to the bar. After we were seated and ordered our drinks, I shifted sideways to face my friend and scan the room's interior. The music, usually a mix of country western and rock, filled the room via some overhead speakers. An upbeat two-step was playing and the dance floor in the corner on the opposite side of the room was full of couples spinning and moving to the beat.

"My name's Derrick," the bartender said and set our drinks, a beer for me and a margarita for Berkley, on the counter. His hair, the color of beach sand, was layered away from his face, the soft curls lightly brushing over the collar of his buttoned shirt. He was built like a tank with broad shoulders and a thick frame and made me think he could double as the bar's bouncer. He pretty much ignored me, his dark gaze locking on Berkley with appreciative interest. "Please let me know if I can get you anything else."

"We're good, thanks," Berkley flippantly replied and slapped a ten-dollar bill on the counter. She picked up her drink, then dismissed him completely by turning away from the bar.

Derrick pressed his lips together tightly and shot daggers at Berkley's back, then roughly grabbed the money off the counter. Apparently, disappointment wasn't something he experienced frequently.

Being rude was so out of character for Berkley. Normally, she was friendly and outgoing with any man she met. I'd seen her flirt relentlessly whether she was interested in a guy or not. "He was cute, and interested." I nudged her arm. "So why the cold-shoulder treatment?"

"Cats are sneaky, devious, and not to be trusted." Berkley stated her belief in a matter-of-fact tone as if it were a written rule.

I glanced over at Derrick, who'd moved to the other

end of the long counter and was talking to another customer. "He's…I never would have guessed." I took a sip of my beer, quickly averting my gaze so Derrick wouldn't catch me staring. Even though he'd worked at the bar for a few years, I didn't know him all that well. On the few occasions I'd chatted with him, he'd always been nice to me. "What kind?"

Berkley sneered. "A mountain lion."

Bad luck with men was one of the things Berkley and I had in common. Though she'd never given me many details, I knew she'd been in a relationship a few years ago. A serious relationship that had ended badly. I couldn't remember Berkley ever expressing a dislike for cats before, not even the domestic kind. Had the guy who'd dumped her been a cat shifter? If he was, it would explain her aversion to getting involved with one.

"The cute cowboy headed this way, however, will do very nicely." Berkley took another sip of her drink, her eyes sparkling with interest.

I followed the direction of her perusal to the man stalking toward us with a confident swagger. His black suede hat was tipped back on his head. He was tall, wore a short-sleeved shirt that accentuated his broad chest, and his jeans clung to a nice set of thick thighs and long legs. Cute was an understatement, and even I had to admit the guy was drool-worthy. Now that I thought about it, a lot of the guys in the bar were lean towers of muscle. Were they also shifters? Had I been living in my own little world for so long that I hadn't noticed? "Is he…"

"Wolf, definitely all wolf." Berkley swiped her tongue across her lower lip as if someone had been dangling a delectable piece of chocolate in front of her.

The guy, wearing a cocky grin, didn't stop until the front of his thighs were inches from Berkley's knees. He gave me a brief glance, then trained his dark gaze on my friend. "Hello, sweet thing. Care to dance?" He held out his hand, his question more of a statement, as if turning him down was not an option.

Berkley swept her hand across her neck, flicking dark chestnut curls behind her back. She let her gaze slowly roam up and down his body, the specks of amber sparkling in her dark brown eyes, then gave him a satisfied smirk. "I'd love to." After draining the rest of her drink, she set the glass on the counter and took his hand. She leaned forward, her tall, shapely frame gliding gracefully from the stool. She winked at me, then held out her hand and let him lead her to the dance floor.

I watched my friend go and envied the way she embraced everything in life. Part of me wished I had Berkley's confidence when it came to men. Another part sat there silently hoping no one would notice me.

The second part of my wish went unnoticed when I heard someone calling my name. I glanced in the direction of the man's voice and smiled at the guy walking toward me. "Adam," I said, taking note of my old friend. He was dressed in a pair of casual slacks and a button-down shirt, and appeared more businesslike and professional than the kid I'd grown up with. His dark hair was cropped short to his head, no longer worn in the straggly shoulder-length style I remembered.

I leaned forward and accepted his hug. "Tired of the big-city life already," I teased and motioned for him to take Berkley's vacated seat. From the time we'd become friends in high school, all Adam had talked about was his dream of becoming a highly paid IT consultant. Five years ago, his determination had paid off, and he'd acquired a great job in Colorado Springs.

"Not quite." He grinned, straddled the stool, and set his drink on the bar. "I'm here on vacation. Came down to see the folks for a few days."

"I'll bet they're glad to have you home."

"Yeah. My dad still refuses to leave town, so it's the only way I get to see them."

I knew a lot of the older residents who'd been born

and raised in Ashbury felt the same way. This was their home. They were comfortable here and had no interest in going anywhere else.

"You're looking good." He didn't bother to hide his appreciative perusal, which lingered a little longer than you'd expect from a casual friend. "How have you been?"

Honestly, this new side of Adam made me a little uncomfortable, and I squirmed on my seat. "Good, staying busy…you know, the usual."

"I was sorry to hear about you and Craig." He flashed me a sympathetic smile. "I never believed what he was telling everyone."

I flinched, remembering the rest of the humiliation that haunted me every time I ran into one of Craig's buddies and had to endure their condescending sneers. The lying asshole had the audacity to tell all his friends—people I'd believed were my friends too—that I'd been the one who'd cheated on him.

Adam reached for my hand and gave it a squeeze. "For the record, I always thought you were too good for him."

"Thanks." Craig was a touchy subject, one I didn't enjoy discussing with anyone. Adam continued to hold my hand, and for the first time, I noticed a hint of desire in his gaze. I'd never been interested in him that way and was sure I never would. I didn't want him to get the wrong impression, so I pulled my hand free and reached for my drink. After taking a long swallow, I glanced down the bar and waved to get Derrick's attention. If this was the direction the rest of my night was headed, I was going to need another drink, maybe several.

NICK

My wolf and I were beyond agitated by the time Reese pulled his truck to a stop next to the jeep parked in the gravel drive. My plans for heading to the bar and finding

Mandy and Berkley were put on hold when we received a call from Bryson Cruise, the bear shifter Reese had hired to patrol the perimeter and check on the cabins located farthest from the lodge. He'd reported that some vandals had broken into one of the unoccupied cabins on the eastern side of our property.

As soon as we got out of the vehicle, Bryson lumbered down the porch steps, the wood creaking under his weight. He was naked and clutching the tattered pieces of what appeared to be his uniform in one hand and his cell phone in the other. I assumed by his appearance that he'd recently shifted and hadn't bothered to take off his clothes first. I'd found myself in similar situations over the years.

"I'm really sorry, boss." Bryson set the items on the hood of truck, then glanced sheepishly between Reese and me. "They were in their vehicle and out of here before I had a chance to catch them. I followed them as far as the border near Bishop's property." He rolled his shoulders, seemingly proud of his endeavor.

Bryson was well over six feet tall, huge for a guy in human form and not a person anyone wanted to mess with. If he'd been able to catch the intruders, I had no doubt he would have caused some serious damage.

"I didn't think it would be a good idea to keep going, but I can if…" Bryson appeared eager about the prospect.

Reese shook his head. "Don't worry about it. You did the right thing by calling us." He frowned at the tree line, then glanced back at me, and I knew what was going through his mind. Hearing that the truck disappeared onto Bishop's land wasn't a surprise to either of us and confirmed our suspicions about the man's involvement. His lust for our land had been a topic of quite a few of our conversations. We knew he was dangerous and had spent quite a bit of time speculating what Bishop's next move might be.

On at least one occasion, Reese had voiced his concern about the crash that had ended our grandfather's life.

According to Reese, who'd been close to James, the old man had spent his entire life in this area and knew every road, trail, and path. The old pickup James had been driving when he died was found at the bottom of a deep ravine, too beat up to tell if it had any help going over the ledge. Though he couldn't prove it, Reese didn't believe it was an accident and suspected Bishop was somehow behind it.

Since using his influence to cut off our local suppliers hadn't worked, it appeared Bishop was trying a more direct approach to shut us down. Damaging our property wouldn't stop us, but having to make additional repairs would be costly and slow down the opening of the resort.

Reese opened his truck door and reached behind the seat. He pulled out a pair of sweats and tossed them to Bryson.

"Appreciate it." Bryson caught them with one hand and quickly tugged them up his legs. The fit was tight, and the length barely reached his ankles.

"Since we're here, why don't you show us the damage?" Reese nodded toward the cabin.

The longer we were here, the more time Mandy was at the bar and around other males. My wolf was growling, anxious to get going. I wasn't thrilled either, but this was important, and I didn't want to let my brother down.

"Most of the damage was done to the plumbing." Bryson took the lead and headed for the porch.

Once inside, Bryson stopped in the kitchen and pointed at the wrench lying on the floor next to the open cabinet underneath the sink. "I don't believe they were expecting me. It looks like they were planning to do a lot more damage but dropped everything when they heard me coming."

The presence of a tool meant the intruders had come prepared. If they'd been regular vandals or teenagers bent on destruction, they would've destroyed the furniture or gone after easier targets like the television sitting on a stand in the corner.

Bryson scratched the stubble covering his chin. "The bathroom was torn up pretty good, but I was able shut off the water and used some of the guest towels to clean up the mess on the floors to save the tile and carpeting."

"Did you get a good look at them?" I asked. I wasn't fond of law enforcement and avoided them as much as possible. If Bryson could recognize those responsible, then maybe we could stop them before they had a chance to do something worse.

Bryson gave a disappointed shrug. "There were two males, and I only saw them from behind. Did catch a scent, though, and they were wolves."

The one advantage to being a wild wolf was the ability to hunt and track better than any of the other breeds. Instead of picking up the wrench, I left it lying on the floor and crouched beside it. After one deep whiff, I was able to get the scent of the person who'd handled it last and logged it into my memory. I moved through the remainder of the cabin, picking up Bryson's scent. Because he'd cleaned in the bathroom, the intruder's scents were faint, harder to detect. It took me a little longer to find an odor for the second man. Now if my path crossed with either of them, I'd recognize them immediately.

We spent the next ten minutes checking the rest of the building and locking everything up. After a few parting words to Bryson, Reese returned me to my cabin. Before I could get out of the vehicle, he turned to me and said, "Why don't you come by the lodge for breakfast in the morning so we can discuss hiring some more security to help Bryson patrol?"

"Sounds good." I quickly exited the vehicle. I would have agreed to pretty much anything if it hurried my brother on his way so I could leave to find Mandy.

CHAPTER SIX

NICK

The music, the low drone of voices, the combined scent of shifters and humans bombarded my senses the instant I walked into the bar. It set my already frustrated wolf on edge, and I paused in the entryway to take several calming breaths.

It wasn't as if I'd never been in a bar before. I had, numerous times, and I knew I could handle it. It was the unsettling need to find Mandy, to be close to her, that was driving my anxiety.

Mate, my wolf countered, his insistence was even greater with the presence of other male shifters in the vicinity.

Glancing around the crowded room, it didn't take me long to spot Berkley out on the dance floor. The guy she was with ignored the music's fast beat. He had his arms wrapped around her waist, their bodies moving slowly, grinding against each other. Not an image of my sister I wanted committed to memory. I had to remind myself she was a grown woman and could take care of herself, something she'd been doing long before I met her.

Our familial relationship might be new, but I couldn't help feeling protective of her. If I didn't know Berkley would rip me a new one, I'd go over there and tell the guy to keep his hands off my baby sister. It didn't mean I wouldn't remain close by in case she needed my help.

After scanning the other faces in the crowd, my wolf and I were relieved that Mandy wasn't one of them. No amount of willpower would have kept me from ripping her out of another man's arms. There were too many smells in the room, but it didn't stop me from trying to lock in on her familiar scent.

I gave the area another scrutinizing scan and finally spotted her sitting on a stool near the bar. Beautiful didn't begin to describe her appearance. All it took was one look and my cock was springing to life. My chest constricted, the tightness making it hard to keep air in my lungs. The top of her jeans rode along her hips, and her sleeveless, silky blue shirt enhanced the color of her eyes. She no longer had her hair confined in a long braid. The shiny golden curls cascaded over her shoulders, a tempting invitation to have my fingers running through them.

I knew I'd been asking for a miracle when I hoped to find her alone. What I hadn't expected was to find a guy sitting next to her, possessively holding her hand. I clenched my fists, fighting to restrain my wolf and the claws slowly descending from my fingertips. I wasn't happy about the raw animalistic powers surging through me or the way my emotions were riding the thin line between jealousy and rage.

In my current state, I didn't have a problem reaching her in record time, humans and shifters alike scattering from my path. They'd either sensed my wolf's push for dominance or had noticed the unnatural hue to my determined gaze.

When I reached Mandy, she was facing away from me and handing the bartender money for the drink he was setting in front of her. It didn't matter that the impeccably dressed man with perfectly combed hair was no longer touching her. Lust had a distinct odor, and he reeked of it. He was sitting too close, and I wanted him gone. "You're in my seat."

"Excuse me." The man jerked his head in my direction, irritation flickering in his dark glare. "What did you say?" The scent of his obvious interest in Mandy was now laced with fear.

"I *said*, you're in my seat." I spat the words more slowly, since the first time, they'd sounded more like a snarl.

"Nick." Mandy glanced over her shoulder, then swiveled on her seat to face me. She widened her eyes, then quickly narrowed them. "What are you doing here?"

Before I could explain, the man interrupted. "Do you know this guy?" He shot her a sidelong glance, keeping most of his attention focused on me.

"Yeah." There was some hesitancy in her voice, and I wasn't sure if she was happy or royally pissed to see me. "Adam, you remember my friend Berkley, right?"

"Old man Reynolds's granddaughter?"

"That's the one." Mandy nodded, her gaze nervously locked with mine. "This is her brother, Nick." By way of an explanation, she added, "I'm working out at the resort now, so technically, he's my boss."

Deciding to use the information to my advantage, I casually crossed my arms and sneered. "Mandy and I have some business to discuss, and maybe it would be best if you leave."

"What?" Adam jutted out his chin, seemingly able to find his spine again. "She's not at work, and you have no right to order us around."

No, I didn't, nor did I care. My only concern was getting Mandy away from the other male. "Whatever it is you're offering, she's not interested." I glanced at Adam's crotch, then back to his reddening face, certain he'd understood my insinuation.

"What makes you think I'm not interested?" Mandy glared at me defiantly.

"Are you?" Adam asked.

I should have known she wasn't going to make this easy. Since I'd already determined from her scent that she had no interest in Adam, I grinned, intent on calling her bluff. "Well, are you?" I quirked a brow, daring her to lie.

Mandy clamped her lips into a tight line and resignedly shook her head. "I'm sorry, Adam, but no, I'm not." She patted his hand. "It was good seeing you again, but maybe you should go."

Rejection is not something any guy wants to hear, and I almost felt bad for Adam when he cringed and his expectant gaze deflated. "Okay, but I'd still like to take you out for dinner while I'm here. You can reach me at my folks' if you change your mind." Adam slid off the stool, leveled an angry glare in my direction, then shouldered his way past me.

As soon as he disappeared, Mandy crossed her arms and pinned me with a murderous stare. I wasn't sure if my chances with her were going to be any better.

MANDY

It had been good to see Adam again, but I couldn't say I was sad to see him disappear into the crowd.

Under different circumstances, I'd be flattered by Nick's interruption and wouldn't be ignoring the heat smoldering throughout my body. It was the pushy way he'd made his point, acting as if I was his personal property, that had me fuming. And there was no way I was going to let him get away with it. I tucked my arms tightly across my chest and focused my simmering anger on Nick.

At least his eyes had returned to their normal color and weren't doing the glowing wolfy thing anymore. "What is wrong with you?" I snapped the minute he straddled the seat Adam had vacated. "You can't walk in here and be rude to people. Adam is my friend. I've known him since high school."

"Your *friend* wanted to get you into bed." Nick flared his nostrils, mirroring the set of my arms with his own. "Was I wrong in assuming you weren't interested?"

"That's beside the point." I didn't want to argue, but I could feel my temper rising along with the heat on my cheeks. "You hardly know me and don't get to make those kinds of decisions for me." I should have been afraid he'd wolf out again like he did in the cabin, but I didn't care. I was really pissed, and I wanted him to know it.

"Mandy, I..." Nick stammered.

"You know what? Never mind." I abandoned my new drink and slid off the stool, then tried to slip past him.

He gently grasped my wrist and kept me in place. "Where are you going?" Suddenly, the arrogance was gone and he appeared lost, vulnerable, as if he was unsure how to go about explaining his actions.

I ignored the warmth radiating from his touch or how much I was enjoying the contact. "To find Berkley and ask her to take me home." It was a weak statement that lacked conviction.

"Please don't leave." He lowered his gaze and made small circles on the back of my hand with his thumb. "I'm not good with people and..."

"Then why did you come here of all places?" Even though his slow caress made it hard for me to concentrate, I needed to know.

He slowly raised his head, honesty gleaming in his silver-gray gaze. "To see you."

I wasn't sure what to say to that, so I remained silent. Berkley had already told me her brother avoided humans and was pretty much a loner. For him to openly admit to being antisocial, that being in a room filled with people was going to be a problem, and yet he still had done it for me had to mean something, didn't it?

The apologetic way he looked at me as if he was drowning and I was the only available life vest tugged at my heart. I couldn't resist his pleading gaze or his adorable half smile, and figured I could meet him halfway. "Okay, I'll stay, but I have two conditions."

Nick straightened his shoulders and grinned. "Name it."

"No more doing the wolf thing with your eyes." I waved my hand in front of his face.

"And the second thing?"

I wanted to make sure he didn't get the wrong impression and believed he could bully someone else. I used the most chastising voice possible. "You have to be polite to my friends. No more chasing them off."

"Even if I can smell that their intentions are less than honorable?" Nick tapped the side of his nose.

"You can..." Of course, he could. He was part wolf. It meant that earlier today when I was practically drooling all over him, he'd scented it. Unsure if I wanted to laugh or cry, I hung my head and blew out an embarrassed breath.

"Mandy."

I braced myself, prepared to endure further humiliation. "What?" I raised my gaze and found him calmly staring at me.

"I'll try."

It took me a few seconds to realize he was referring to my stipulations. "Okay." I returned to my seat and took a long swig of the beer. "Do you want something to drink?" I raised my hand to signal Derrick. Maybe if we were both drinking—a lot—I'd be able to forget what I'd recently discovered.

He pulled my hand from the air and held it in his lap. "What would you say to getting out of here? Going someplace where it isn't so loud." My quizzical look had him adding, "It wasn't a proposition. I thought maybe we could go into town and get a coffee, an ice cream, or anything you want." He squeezed my hand. "Then afterward, I'll take you home."

I wondered if he realized how boyishly charming his request sounded. Between work and taking care of my father, it had been a while since I'd done something so casual and fun. "Ice cream sounds great." I slid off my stool again. "I need to find Berkley first and let her know I'm leaving."

"Not a problem." Nick stood and pulled his cell phone out of his back pocket, then typed something on the screen.

Curious, I asked, "Who are you texting?"

"Berkley. I'm letting her know that I'm taking you home."

"Oh," I mumbled. Not only was he handsome as hell, but he deserved a gold star for ingenuity. I glanced toward the dance floor and, sure enough, within seconds, Berkley was reaching into her back pocket. She looked at the small screen, then glanced in our direction and shot us a wide grin as she waved good-bye.

Once we were in Nick's truck, I snapped the seat belt into place and gave him a sidelong glance. I leaned back against the headrest with an amused smile. Maybe letting Berkley talk me into going to the bar hadn't been such a bad idea after all.

CHAPTER SEVEN

NICK

I couldn't deny my growing attraction to Mandy or how badly I wanted to have her naked beneath me, writhing with need and screaming my name as I thrust into her. The way I'd scared off Adam hadn't scored me any points. If anything, it guaranteed she wouldn't ever speak to me again. I couldn't blame my irrational behavior on my wolf, and I sure as hell couldn't tell her she might be my mate. *Is our mate*, my wolf growled.

Feeling as if I'd gotten a reprieve, I had no problem agreeing to her stipulations, not if it meant she'd forgive me. I couldn't believe I'd followed it up with an invitation for ice cream. Why the memory of the quaint little shop I'd seen when I'd first arrived in Ashbury had picked that moment to pop into my head, I had no idea. It had to be one of the lamest moves I'd ever made with a woman, but it was the only thing I could think of to get her out of the bar so I could spend more time alone with her.

I wanted to be the one to take her home, but not right away. My stomach clenched into a tight knot, and I wanted to kick myself for suggesting we get a delectable treat after an amused smile formed on her lips. I was certain she'd tell me "no," or worse, laugh in my face. Instead, she'd happily agreed, and I'd nearly fallen off my stool.

It hadn't taken us long to drive the busy stretch of road between the bar and Ashbury. Friday night in the small town was no different from any other city in the country. People who'd spent the week working hard finally had a chance to get out, relax, and have some fun. Cars occupied the spots in front of the shop along the town's main street, so I had to park my truck two blocks away from our intended destination.

I wasn't completely without manners. Things might have been tough growing up, but my mother made sure I understood the right way to act around people when I was younger. I dashed around the front of the vehicle, getting to Mandy's door in time to open it for her. Being independent, I'd expected an argument, not the beaming smile I received when she took my offered hand.

As soon as she slid from the vehicle, her foot missed the curb and she fell into my arms. "Sorry." She gripped my shoulders to right herself, her breasts pushing into my chest, her stomach pressing against my groin.

I took the time to inhale her feminine scent. A scent belonging to her alone. "No problem. Are you okay?" I was instantly hard and suppressed a growl, hoping she hadn't noticed how her nearness was affecting me. I loosened my grip but kept my hands on her hips longer than I should have. I knew it was wrong, but I could see where her penchant for accidents could play in my favor.

"Fine, thanks." She glanced at the ground, moving to the side and making sure her next step connected with the sidewalk.

"Feel free to throw yourself at me anytime." I closed the door and pressed my hand to the small of her back, guiding her in the direction of the shop.

She chuckled. "I'll keep it in mind."

My legs were longer and my strides faster, so I took

smaller steps, falling into an easy pace with Mandy. Even though the street lamps lit up the area, I got glimpses of the star-filled evening sky as we walked. The other couples we passed were deep in conversation and seemed oblivious to our presence.

She shuddered, then, to my surprise, tucked her arm through mine and leaned into me as we moved along the sidewalk. "You're really warm." She gazed up at me and smiled. "You don't mind, do you?"

Hell no. I hadn't noticed that there was a slight chill in the air, mainly because it didn't bother me. Because of my wolf, my temperature always ran a little warmer.

"Not at all." For the first time today, the uneasy tightness in my gut was gone and my wolf was calm. If the animal could purr, he'd be rumbling loudly.

I'd never been a great communicator, mostly because I didn't care what other people had to say. With Mandy, it was different. I wanted to know everything about her, had plenty of questions, but didn't know where to start. Lucky for me, she didn't have the same problem.

"Berkley told me you lived in California. Do you miss it?"

"Not really." I placed my hand over hers, stopping at the end of the sidewalk and waiting for the pedestrian light to turn green signaling it was okay for us to cross the street to the next block. "I moved around a lot and didn't get a chance to call any particular place home."

"And now?" She glanced at the ground before stepping off the curb. "Are you planning to make this your home, or will you be leaving soon?" There was more than curiosity in her tone; somehow, I sensed my answer really mattered to her.

"I haven't decided. I promised Berkley I'd give it a year. After that…" I didn't know. It was the truth, though the more time I spent with my siblings, and now Mandy, the more I could see myself settling down here. Having a real home for the first time in my life.

"Oh." Her smile faded, and there was a note of disappointment in her voice.

Would she miss me if I suddenly decided to leave? Talking about myself was not a subject I enjoyed, and I wanted the smile to return to her face. "What about you? Have you lived anywhere else, done any traveling?"

"I grew up in Ashbury and never made it out of the state. I've gone to Denver a few times, and Hanford is the farthest east I've ever been."

"Berkley said you've known each other a long time. How did you meet?" I asked.

She wrinkled her nose, and her step faltered as if my question somehow troubled her. "You don't have to tell me if you'd rather not."

"It's kind of a long story," Mandy said.

"We have plenty of time."

"Okay, then." She spent the next five minutes telling me about her experience. By the time she finished, we were standing in front of the ice cream shop. I was glad my sister had been there for her all those years ago. If I had been the one to intercede, the two boys who'd terrorized Mandy would have returned home beaten and bloodied.

"Shall we?" I cut a path between the six round metal tables with matching chairs that took up a wide section of the sidewalk. Each table had a blue-and-yellow umbrella attached to a tall pole mounted to its center. I opened the door, letting Mandy enter ahead of me. It appeared that quite a few people had the same idea, because there was a line extending down the main aisle in front of us.

"We can go somewhere else if you'd rather not stay," Mandy said.

"It's fine. I promised you ice cream, and waiting doesn't bother me." I grinned and placed my arm around the back of her waist. "Besides, you're the one who's going to have to put up with me a lot longer."

She patted my chest. "I'm pretty sure I can handle it."

Yep, there was surely going to be purring.

The line disappeared sooner than I thought it would, and we found ourselves standing in front of the counter being greeted by a tall and lanky, freckle-faced teenage boy. "What'll ya have," he said through a thick mouthful of braces as he dipped a metal scoop into a small container of water.

"I'll have one scoop of the mint chip with extra hot fudge topping." Mandy pointed at the half-empty tub of pale green ice cream sprinkled with bits of chocolate.

"Extra chocolate, huh? Do you have a sweet tooth?" I asked.

"You have no idea." She giggled. "I'm still holding out hope that chocolate makes it into one of the recommended food groups."

Nick glanced back at the attendant. "I'll have the same, but make mine three scoops and double the extra hot fudge."

Mandy rolled her eyes at me. "What were you saying about a sweet tooth?"

"Guilty."

In no time, the attendant had finished, and I paid for our order. "Why don't we sit outside?" I snatched the ice-cream filled containers off the counter.

"Sounds like a plan." Mandy grinned, grabbed two Styrofoam cups filled with ice and water, then headed for the door.

There were a couple of empty tables available inside, but I had an ulterior motive for wanting to sit outside. Hopefully, Mandy would be a little more chilled after eating her ice cream and wouldn't mind snuggling up against me some more.

There is a reason wolves have a reputation for being devious.

MANDY

Don't get attached, don't get attached, don't get attached. Being with Nick was easy, fun, and way too comfortable. And I didn't want to listen to my inner voice's warning or consider the possibility that one day, he might decide to leave.

I saw him gazing with interest at the remainder of my ice cream, and I encircled the cardboard dish protectively with my hand. "Don't even think about it." I waved the pink plastic spoon I held in my other hand in front of his face. "You already had three scoops. How can you still be hungry?"

Nick grinned. "I was trying to impress you with my willpower. Usually I have five."

I laughed, glancing at his lean muscles and wondering if a high metabolism was a shifter thing or a Nick thing. I thought about asking him but didn't get the chance. My thoughts were interrupted by the two men who'd stopped next to our table. A prickly sensation skittered along my neck, and I raised my gaze to take a look, then wished I hadn't. They were sneering at Nick, and I got the distinct impression they were here to cause trouble.

I couldn't remember their names but recognized their faces. They worked for Desmond Bishop, the owner of the Hanford Regency, a recently constructed luxury hotel near the city it was named after. My father never said why, but he refused to do any work for the man and had warned me to stay clear of him.

Both were dressed in short-sleeved button-down shirts and jeans. They were tall, maybe a few inches shorter than Nick, and had similarly thick arms, as if they'd spent most of their time working out in a gym. What caught my attention most was their cocky, confident stance. It reminded me a lot of the cowboy Berkley had been dancing with in the bar. The only difference between these two and him was the dangerous gleam in their dark eyes. A gleam that had me scooting my chair a little closer to Nick's.

The one standing closest to me smacked the other man on the arm with the back of his hand. "Dale, can you believe Reese let his brother off his leash?"

So this was personal. Nick had his arm draped across the back of my chair, and I felt his muscles tense. I gave him an indirect glance, noting how tightly he clamped his jaw and the way his other hand was fisted against his thigh. I didn't see any fangs, but I had a feeling it wouldn't be long before his wolf pushed to the surface.

Dale snickered. "Maybe he hasn't learned that wild animals don't belong around beautiful women." He licked his lips, letting his lustful gaze linger on my breasts. It was unnerving and made my skin itch. I resisted the urge to cross my arms to block his view.

"Take your eyes off my..." Nick snarled, narrowing his gaze.

His what? I didn't have time to contemplate what he'd been about to say. Nick was pushing his chair away from the table, the metal scraping loudly across the sidewalk's concrete surface. I was certain Nick could take care of himself in a fight, but two against one wasn't fair odds. Besides, I didn't want to see him get hurt and needed to find a way to defuse the situation, and fast.

I also remembered my father's warning and was suddenly afraid of what Desmond Bishop would do once he learned Nick had tangled with his men. "Don't. They're not worth it," I pleaded, gripping Nick's arm and urging him to remain seated.

He slowly settled back in his chair, his intense glare never leaving the two men. He pressed his head near my face and whispered, "For you, anything."

I released the breath I hadn't realized I'd been holding. I had hoped Dale and his buddy would take the hint and leave, but no such luck. It didn't matter what I said, they were determined to provoke Nick into a fight.

"Why don't you come with me, pretty thing? I'll show you how much better I am than this worthless half-breed." Dale licked his lips again.

That was it. Nick was growling again, and I'd had all I could take of these two idiots, their badgering, and of Dale staring at my breasts. I wasn't stupid enough to get into a verbal confrontation, so I searched for something I could use as a distraction. I noticed how close my cup of water was sitting to the napkin dispenser and decided it would work nicely for what I had in mind.

It didn't take much effort for me to make it look like an accident when I reached for a napkin and my hand *accidentally* brushed the side of the cup, knocking it over. Water splashed across the table, over the edge, and right down the front of Dale's pants.

"What the…" Dale jumped backward and growled, elbowing his friend in the process.

Not only was he wet, but the water had been cold. I had to bite my lip to keep from smiling when I saw that some of the ice hadn't melted and was sitting in the puddle on the table. "Oh, my gosh. I'm so sorry." Though I didn't mean a word of it, my gushed apology sounded sickly sweet.

"You did that on purpose, you little…" Dale took a menacing step toward me, then stopped when two couples exited the shop. They gave Dale and his friend a wary glance, then headed for the empty table sitting farthest away from us.

"Leave it and let's go." Dale's buddy nudged him, obviously not wanting to draw any more attention.

"Fine." Dale shrugged away from him, then glared at Nick. "This isn't over, Pearson."

I waited until they were out of hearing distance, then turned to face Nick. "What did he mean this isn't over?"

"Nothing you need to worry about." He brushed his hand across my cheek and tucked some loose strands behind my ear.

Of course, I was going to worry, but I refrained from saying anything. "They were shifters, weren't they?" I made sure to keep my voice low so the people at the nearby table couldn't hear me.

"Yeah, wolves," Nick said absently, continuing to stare after the two men until they'd gotten into a vehicle parked down the street and driven away.

There were obviously more shifters living in Ashbury than Berkley had led me to believe. I was going to have a serious talk with my friend the next time I saw her. With my strong attraction to Nick, it also brought up the question of whether shifters had more than the friendship kind of relationships. The kinds that were long-lasting, more precisely, the ones with humans. Other than the turning-into-an-animal thing—a big deal by itself—as far as I knew, shifters' lives were pretty much the same as anyone else's.

Would I be wasting my time? Should I even be contemplating the possibility of getting to know Nick better, that our interest was mutual and could lead to something more? Nick wasn't sure if he was going to be sticking around. Did I really want to put my heart out there only to get it broken again?

"I'm sorry about that." Nick placed his hand on my thigh. "Are you okay?"

I snapped out of my musing and met his gaze, concern darkening his furrowed brow.

"I'm fine. It's not the first time I've had to deal with bullies." I placed my hand over his and gave it a reassuring squeeze. "Nick, you need to be careful. Those men work for Desmond Bishop and he's…dangerous."

"Are you worried about me?" He seemed elated by the notion and gave me a lopsided grin.

"I'm more worried about what Berkley would do if something happened to that handsome face of yours," I teased.

"So you think I'm handsome?"

Unbelievable, arrogant wolf. "No, I…"

He captured my hand before I could pull it away. "Thanks."

A rush of heat spread across my cheeks again. "For what?" I wasn't sure if he was still talking about the compliment.

"For the trick with the water and keeping me from losing control."

"Are you going to tell me what that was all about?" I asked.

"Maybe some other time. Why don't I get you home before we get into any more trouble?"

"Sure." For once, I wasn't anxious to go home, and reluctantly pushed away from the table. I let him take my hand and lead me toward his truck, wishing the whole time that the evening would end with one or both of us getting naked—together.

CHAPTER EIGHT

NICK

I leaned on the edge of the lateral cabinet pressed against the far wall in Reese's office and crossed my longs legs at the ankles. It was midmorning by the time I was able to get Berkley to drag her ass out of bed and join Reese and me for our meeting to discuss additional security for the resort.

While we waited for Berkley to get her much-needed coffee, I replayed the previous night over in my head, at least the parts that involved Mandy. I'd almost said "mate," almost divulged to her and the males working for Bishop about her connection to me. My protective instincts were shouting loudly that her safety could be at risk if they knew what she meant to me. As for Mandy, the fear of rejection was strong. It was part of the reason I was hiding behind denial and the reason I wasn't willing to tell her.

She knew about shifters and seemed comfortable with me being one, more than comfortable if I took the time to analyze the situation. It was unclear whether she was aware of the wild wolf side of my nature. Would she accept that part of me as well, or would she avoid me like so many others had once they found out?

Any further contemplation was interrupted by Berkley treading barefoot across the hardwood floor. She still wore her oversized purple night shirt with paw prints all over it and had thrown on a pair of wrinkled sweats underneath. Even the state of her hair was haphazard, having been fastened behind her head in a ponytail.

Noting the darkened skin beneath her eyes and the way she protectively clutched her mug, it wasn't hard to assume she hadn't gotten much sleep. She ignored Reese's questioning look, pushed aside a stack of papers, then hopped on top of his desk. After crossing her legs in front of her, she shifted so she was facing both of us.

"Rough night, sis?" Reese frowned at the mess she'd made of his organized files.

"Back off." She snarled and flicked her hand, extending her claws at him threateningly.

Reese snorted, ignored her warning, and leaned back in his chair. I watched their interaction, secretly amused. I'd have thought with all his military training Reese would know better than to antagonize our sister before she'd had her fill of caffeine. Or maybe irritating her was his way of showing affection.

After taking a long sip, she glanced between Reese and me, then asked, "What was so important that you couldn't let me sleep a little longer?"

Reese tapped his fingertips together. "Someone broke into one of the cabins along the eastern perimeter last night."

"How bad?" Berkley pursed her lips, her grip on the cup tightening.

"Some minor plumbing. Bryson chased them off before they could do any major damage," Reese said.

"We should hire more security," she said.

"That's what we thought as well. I know someone from my old unit who does contract work and might be willing to help."

"Any clues yet as to who's behind it?" Berkley took a sip from her cup, then released a low moan of appreciation. "Do you think it was some of the local teens?"

"No. We're sure it was planned. We found a wrench they'd left behind."

"Any likely suspects?" Berkley was well aware of my superior tracking abilities and glanced in my direction expecting an answer.

"That's what I wanted to talk to you about. I ran into the guys…" A rap on the door stopped me from telling my siblings about the run-in I'd had with Dale and his buddy the night before.

"Come in." Reese leaned forward in his chair, the old leather squeaking under his weight.

Nina, the young woman Reese had hired to answer phones and perform administrative duties, stood in the doorway, nervously wringing her hands. She was a sweet kid, barely older than twenty. "I'm sorry to interrupt." Her gaze went straight to Reese. "There is a Mr. Bishop here to see you. He doesn't have an appointment but refuses to leave until he speaks to you."

Reese glanced at Berkley and me, silently asking our permission. After we both nodded, he spoke to Nina. "It's fine. Show him in."

"Okay." The tension in Nina's shoulders disappeared with a sag. She nodded, then retreated from the room.

"This ought to be interesting," Reese said once Nina was out of sight.

A couple of minutes later, the sound of heavy footsteps echoed in the hall, and Nina appeared in the doorway again. "In here." She stepped aside, her shorter, more slender frame dwarfed by Desmond's presence. The man was all business as he strolled into the office wearing a gray pin-striped suit complete with a burgundy silk tie.

I knew that Reese and Berkley had dealt with Desmond

on several occasions and seemed surprised to see the two men accompanying him. I, on the other hand, was ready to shed blood. I'd recognized their scents the night before when they'd stopped to hassle Mandy and me at the ice cream shop.

They were the two wolves who'd damaged the cabin. If I'd been alone at the time, my wolf and I would have handled things a lot differently. My need to keep Mandy safe and off their radar was the only reason they were still walking. Though I still held out hope that I'd get my hands on Dale, the scumbag on the left, so I could hurt him slowly and painfully for ogling and threatening Mandy.

Dale and his buddy froze a few feet into the room, shooting angry glares in my direction and letting me know they weren't happy to see me either. Reese focused his piercing gaze on the two men before returning his attention to Desmond. No doubt he'd recognized their scents as well and was doing a good job concealing the fact.

"I appreciate you taking the time to meet with me." Desmond continued into the office and held out his hand.

Their uninvited visitors were the enemy, and Reese didn't bother to stand or return the gesture of greeting. It was a clear sign of disrespect, one that didn't go unnoticed by Desmond. He lowered his hand to his side, his fake smile losing some of its luster.

"Who are the goons?" Berkley directed the question at Desmond.

"These are my associates. This is Dale." He pointed to the male on the left, then to the other on the right. "And Carl."

"Whatever," Berkley muttered, then snubbed them by rolling her eyes and continuing to sip her coffee.

"What do you want, Bishop?" Reese got straight to the point.

"The same thing I've always wanted: to make you a generous offer on the resort." Desmond made himself comfortable in the chair opposite Reese's desk. Carl and Dale positioned themselves behind him, their rigid stances meant as a show of force.

"You could have called and saved yourself the trip." Reese crossed his arms. "We're still not interested."

"How do you know if you haven't even heard what I'm willing to pay?"

"The resort is not for sale for any amount of money," Reese countered.

"You're even more stubborn than your grandfather, and look what that got him." His face was masked in calm, but there was a hint of frustration in his voice. "The place is falling apart. Wouldn't you rather spend your money on something more profitable?"

"What we do with our money is none of your concern." Reese tapped the edge of his desk. "And in case I didn't make myself clear the first time, we're not interested in selling."

"But since you're here…" I braced my hands on the cabinet. "Mind telling us what your guys were doing breaking into one of our cabins last night?"

Desmond slowly curled one side of his lips into a sneer. "Surely you aren't insinuating that I would do anything unlawful to gain ownership of the resort?"

"I don't need to insinuate. You might want to hire better help the next time you send your *boys* to damage our property. They're sloppy and left their scent all over the place." As I'd hoped, my comment hit a nerve. Desmond's flinch, along with the tic in the muscle of his jaw, was more noticeable.

"Your brother's got you back on your leash again, I see," Dale smarted off, too stupid to realize this was the wrong place to provoke me. "Where's that pretty little girlfriend of yours?"

Yep, too stupid. I released a low, feral growl and cracked my knuckles. The hurting was going to start sooner rather than later.

Dale and Carl lacked their boss's self-control. They snarled, baring fangs and extending their claws.

Desmond kept his attention focused on me and held up his hand, a warning to his underlings. "Rein it in. This is a friendly meeting. We didn't come here looking for trouble." He waited for the men to calm down and take a step back. "I'm sure you're mistaken. If they were involved in your mishap, and I'm not saying they were…good luck proving it."

The man was all kinds of smarmy and gave shifters a bad name. My wolf was in total agreement with gutting the bastard before he had a chance to leave the room. Mental images of the best places my animal considered hiding a corpse flipped through my mind. Of course, I'd never take a life without provocation, but I couldn't help appreciating my wolf's simplistic way of wanting to deal with things.

Desmond pushed out of his chair, casting one last glance at the three of us. "You really should consider taking my offer. This place is old, and there's no telling what kind of accidents might happen."

The man had a pair of brass ones to toss that kind of threat at us in our own home. Before I could voice my opinion, Reese got to his feet and pointed toward the door. "I'm sure you can find your way out."

Desmond reached inside his jacket and retrieved a business card. He placed it on the desk, tapping it with his finger. "We'll be talking again soon." He inclined his head toward Carl and Dale, then left the room with them trailing behind him.

I pushed away from the cabinet, intent on following them.

"Nick, where are you going?" Reese stepped in front of me and blocked my path to the doorway.

I didn't miss the concern lining my brother's face and knew he was wondering if I was going to lose it. "Stop worrying. My wolf's under control. I just want to make sure our unwanted guests don't have any problem leaving the property."

CHAPTER NINE

MANDY

Two days had passed since my semi-date with Nick at the ice cream shop. And just like the day before, I'd set my alarm to buzz an hour sooner than normal with the intention of arriving at the resort early. I told myself the reason I'd spent the extra time fixing my hair and laboring over my decision to find the perfect shirt had nothing to do with the possibility of seeing Nick.

There was no reason I couldn't look nice to do my job, was there?

After my initial disappointment of finding his truck missing from his driveway, I drove to the next cabin scheduled for repairs. Except for exchanging the vanity in Nick's bathroom—the new one to replace the cracked one I'd ordered—I'd finished all the work required in his home the day before.

This cabin was going to be a lot easier since some of the metal piping had already been replaced with PVC. After hopping out of the vehicle, I grabbed my toolbox and headed inside to the bathroom, where I settled in and got to work. Two hours and a few scrapes later, I was almost finished. I laid my wrench on top of the counter next to the sink and grabbed a clean rag from my stash. I wiped the grime from my hands, then took a step back to admire my handiwork. Once I turned on the water and made sure there were no leaks, I could start in the kitchen.

Thinking about water made me thirsty. I realized I'd left the cooler in the front of my truck and decided now was a good time to go get it. After stopping in the kitchen to wash my hands, I pushed open the squeaky screen and paused. Nick, dressed in a snug-fitting black T-shirt and worn jeans, was sitting on the porch, his legs hanging over the edge. He was amazingly handsome, and I reacted accordingly with a racing heart and a slow simmering heat that scorched every part of my body.

I'd learned from Berkley that Nick had been spending most of his time doing errands for Reese. Other than a few waves from a distance, I hadn't spoken to him since he'd delivered me to the front porch of my father's house two nights ago.

My lips still warmed at the memory of the gentle kiss he'd placed on them before leaving. It had left me aching with need and wanting more. Too bad my father had been home; otherwise, I'd have been tempted to break my rule about sleeping with a guy before really getting to know him and dragged Nick inside and upstairs to my bedroom.

Nick being here didn't necessarily mean anything. Since I worked for him and his family, he was probably stopping by to check on my progress. Though if that was the case, wouldn't he have come inside?

Before I could continue arguing with myself, Nick glanced over his shoulder, his smile growing brighter. "Hey, there."

One look from those silvery-gray eyes had me melting. "Hey back." I realized I was gawking and still had my hand pressed against the doorframe. "What are you doing here?" I returned his smile, then curiously stepped onto the porch.

"I thought I'd surprise you." He patted the spot next to him. "You're due for a break, right?"

"Yeah, I suppose so." I squatted down next to him and swung my legs over the edge.

"Good, because I brought you something." He reached to his right where he'd hidden a square, white plastic container sealed with a lid. Grinning like a kid with a Christmas gift, he handed it to me.

"Thanks." It was small and fit perfectly on my lap. "What is it?" I stared at the opaque finish, hoping to get a glimpse inside.

"Guess you'll have to open it and see."

I inhaled his musky scent, a mixture of sandalwood and the forest after a rain shower. Having him this close made it hard for me to breathe, let alone maintain a clear thought, and I fumbled with the lid. Nick scooting closer, his thigh pressed against mine, wasn't helping my concentration issue. After an embarrassing amount of struggling, I finally got one corner undone.

"Need some help?"

Yes. "No, I've got it." I removed the rest of the lid without dumping the whole thing on the ground. Inside was a blueberry Danish, huge in comparison to anything I'd ever purchased from a store. A thick layer of white icing was spread across the top and dripped down the sides. The smell was overpoweringly delicious and made my mouth water. I was surprised he'd remembered my sweet tooth and gone out of his way to bring me something special. "This looks awesome." I gazed at him curiously. "And homemade. Did you make it?"

"Nah, my talents lie elsewhere." Nick wiggled his brows. "Berkley was baking, and I stole it when she wasn't looking." He appeared pleased with his admission about his thieving abilities.

"She does love to cook and bake." I'd learned about my friend's passion years ago after Berkley coerced me into tasting anything she'd created in the kitchen.

"And she's really good at it, but don't tell her I told you." Nick grinned. "I'll never hear the end of it."

I giggled and glanced at my treat. "No fork?"

"Sorry, fingers only. I was in fear for my life, so I had to perform a snatch-and-escape operation."

"Who am I to deny a man who is willing to risk death to bring me such a magnificent morsel?" I picked up one end of the Danish, my thumb and forefinger squishing into the thick icing. After taking a bite, I briefly closed my eyes and enjoyed how the sweet mixture of soft bread and blueberries melted on my tongue. I moaned softly, then glanced at Nick, ready to thank him, and stopped when I noticed the hungry way he was staring at my mouth. "What?" I swallowed hard and nervously licked my lips.

"You missed some." He slid his thumb along my lower lip, coming away with a dab of icing, which he slowly sucked into his mouth. A mouth I couldn't stop staring at. My nipples hardened, and warmth pooled between my legs. I wished he was giving parts of my body the same attention he was giving his thumb.

He released a low rumble, then leaned forward and brushed his mouth across mine, swiping my lip with his tongue. "Hmm. Very tasty."

I shuddered, wondering what it would be like to have him kiss me. Not a brush of his mouth over mine, but a full-blown, passionate kiss. Seconds later, I got my wish and nearly dropped the remainder of the Danish. Nick grasped me by the nape to anchor me in place and captured my mouth with his. What started out playful and teasing turned into a possessively dominating kiss with tongues entwined and both of us moaning.

When he finally released me, there was mischief in his gaze, and he was panting as hard as I was. "There." He smirked. "I think I got it all." He ran his finger along my hand where it rested on the edge of the container and gripped the Danish. "You should have another bite."

I'd been so distracted by his kiss, I was surprised I'd

been able to maintain my grasp. "Why do I get the feeling the only reason you brought me this Danish was so you could lick the icing off my lips?"

Nick chuckled, holding up his hands in mock innocence. "I swear I didn't have any ulterior motives at the time, but I won't say I'm unhappy about the results."

"Really?" Unable to resist his challenging gaze and interested to see what he'd do next, I set the Danish aside and slowly raised the finger coated with icing to my lips. With lightning-quick speed, he snagged my hand and sucked the tip into his mouth. He twirled his tongue across my skin, the sensation so intimate, so heated, that I was certain I was going to melt.

His pupils widened with desire as he gave my thumb the same amount of attention, slowly lapping the pad, then sucking it into his mouth. He reached for me again, this time pulling me across his lap. He caught my lower lip with his teeth and gently tugged, then swiped his tongue across my lower lip, plunging deeper and taking control.

I gasped and slid my hands along his shoulders, entwining my fingers in the hair at his nape. I'd never had anyone turn a kiss into such an erotic event and didn't want him to stop.

NICK

Icing or not, Mandy tasted even better than I'd imagined, and I couldn't get enough of her. It had been extremely hard for me to give her one chaste kiss two nights ago when I'd dropped her off at home. I'd spent the rest of the evening tossing and turning, dreaming about her, wanting and needing more.

I'd planned to spend the following day doing repair work around my cabin so I could be near her, could spend time with her. Reese, of course, had other plans for me. As much as I wanted to argue with my brother, I couldn't. I'd agreed to pull my weight when it came to the renovations and managing the resort. Coordinating supply deliveries and discussing the new candidates for security needed to be addressed immediately. Bishop and his determination to obtain the resort was a real threat, one we couldn't afford to dismiss.

My erection was straining against the inside of my pants, and if I had my way, I'd drag Mandy back to my cabin and spend the rest of the day exploring every inch of her beautiful body. Though I'd finally agreed with my wolf that she was our mate, I'd been battling the persistent animal for the past two days.

My wolf was pushing me hard to claim her and didn't understand what I was waiting for, why I was taking things slowly. Mandy was human, and I wasn't sure if she understood what it meant to be a mate, to commit to one another permanently, to seal our bond forever. Couple that with my wild nature, the kind of life I'd lived—the complete opposite of hers—and things couldn't get any more complicated.

Having been alone for so long, I'd never allowed myself to get emotionally involved with anyone else. For the first time in my life, I was considering what it would be like to take a chance and let myself care about someone so deeply that it would hurt if I lost them. I was trying to reach the point where I wasn't battling my own reservations about the whole lifetime thing and didn't want to risk chasing Mandy off in the process.

Berkley with her persistence and Reese with his unconditional acceptance of my wolf had gone a long way to changing my mind. In the short time I'd known Mandy, she'd broken through the barrier protecting my heart in a way I'd never thought possible.

I stared at the woman whose ice-blue gaze shimmered with mischief. When she'd taunted me by trying to lick the icing from her finger, I hadn't been able to stop myself from going after the sweet confection again. I'd wanted her closer, so rather than lean toward her again I'd tugged her onto my lap sideways and encircled her waist with my arms.

When I pulled away panting, I stared at her lips again, now swollen from my ministrations. "I like this much better, but I'll need another taste."

"You will, huh?" she murmured.

"Absolutely." After dipping my finger in the icing on the Danish, I dabbed it on her lip, then swiped my tongue across the soft surface, moving side to side and wiping away the layer and tasting the sweetness below. She moaned, opening for me, allowing me to delve deeper to show her the extent of my passion. What I really wanted was to shift her so she was straddling me and I could grind my erection between her legs. The more we played our tasting game, the more we kissed, the more my cock strained uncomfortably inside my pants.

Mandy was the first to pull out of our kiss, worry creasing her brow. She tilted her head to the side. "Did you hear that?"

I hadn't heard anything, not until she'd brought it to my attention. I'd been too focused on the scent of her arousal and the soft moans she'd been making during our kisses to pay attention to anything happening around us. I jerked my head in the direction she was staring and detected an animal's whimper.

She scooted off my lap and walked to the end of the porch where the ground sloped toward the crawlspace underneath. "There's something under here."

"Mandy, wait. Don't go under there," I ordered when she crouched and disappeared from view. A heavy weight pressed against my chest. My wolf snarled, and I was off the porch and around the corner in seconds. She was on her hands and knees, the front half of her body already slipping into the space created by two of the supporting beams.

"Hey, there," she cooed softly and inched ahead slowly.

"I'm not going to hurt you."

I knelt behind her and sniffed the air, unable to relax when I caught a dog's scent. Her slender form filled the narrow space, and I couldn't see past her to get a glimpse of what was hiding in the shadows. Images of something big and furry with teeth as sharp as my wolf's sifted through my mind, increasing my anxiety. The thought of anything tearing into her soft flesh had my wolf snarling, pushing to shift, prepared to attack.

I gripped her ankle protectively, ready to drag her out at the first sign of trouble. "Mandy, come back out of there and leave it alone before it bites you."

"Nick, it's fine. Just give me a minute." There was a hint of irritation in her determined tone. "Come here, baby." Mandy was talking to the animal again, and I heard her pat the ground several times. "It's okay. Come on." The whimpers grew steadily stronger and closer.

"Got ya," she exclaimed happily, then wiggled her rear and slowly backed toward me.

"Don't ever do that again. Do you know how dangerous it is to mess with..." The admonishment died on my lips when she sat back on her haunches, clutching a small dog that barely covered the front of her chest.

"Poor little thing. Someone probably didn't want him and dumped him out here." Anger flared in her gaze, changing the crystal to a deep blue.

"Does that happen a lot?" I gripped her elbow and helped her stand. I didn't know a lot about dogs but was pretty sure this one would be classified as a mutt. With all the dirt and mud covering its furry coat, it was hard to tell its natural color. The animal had its head tucked against her neck, its whole body shaking. The lack of nourishment was easily evident by the defined ribs beneath the thin layer of fur and skin. Even I couldn't help but feel sympathetic for the cowering creature.

"More than you'd think, though their survival rate isn't very high. It's a good thing we found this little guy when we did; otherwise…" She shuddered, then ran her hand soothingly along the animal's spine. "Come on, killer, let's get you fixed up before the big bad wolf decides to make a snack out of you," Mandy teased, shooting me a reproachful glare, then moving around the porch and heading for her truck.

"Wait, where are you going?" I quickly closed the distance between us and placed my hand on her arm to stop her.

"Up to the lodge. Look at the poor thing, he's starving, and Berkley might have some scraps we can feed him."

I stared at the pathetic little bundle that nuzzled against her neck while keeping one of its eyes warily focused on me. I remembered hearing or reading somewhere that animals were a sure way to a woman's heart. Selfishly, I wanted my wolf to be that animal, but was resigned to giving this four-legged interloper some attention if it meant I'd be able to score some points with Mandy. "Let's take him to my cabin. It's closer."

After ushering Mandy and her bundle into the passenger seat of her truck, it didn't take us long to make the short trip to my place. I followed her onto the porch, then paused with my hand on the door handle. "Just so we're clear, if he or she makes a mess, you're cleaning it up."

"Deal." Mandy sighed, rolling her eyes and shaking her head as she walked inside ahead of me. "We'll need to give him a bath too, but it can wait until after we've fed him."

I dug through the newly stocked food in my refrigerator and found a package of sliced beef I'd used to make sandwiches. Surprisingly, I found myself relating to the dog and what we had in common. I'd been a stray most of my adult life, moving from one job to the next, never staying in one place long, and never having a place I could call home.

Mandy had witnessed the feral nature of my wolf, at least a partial version, and had unconditionally accepted us.

I had no doubt the dog's life had just changed for the better, that she would do everything she could to protect it. Was it possible that, like the furry creature she cradled in her arms, I'd finally found a place where I could belong?

I set the plastic baggie on the counter, and before I could argue, Mandy was shoving the animal into my arms. "Here, why don't you feed him while I run a bath for him?" She headed down the hall and smiled over her shoulder. "There's towels in the closet, right?"

All the cabins had been set up for guests and were stocked with towels and linens. I snagged the pouch and followed her. "You're going to use my bath towels for the dog."

She pulled two towels off the shelf and walked into the bathroom. "Yes, unless you want me to use one of your T-shirts to dry him off." She tugged on the side of her tank top. "Mine doesn't have enough material."

"You're going to be more trouble than your worth, aren't you?" I muttered to the dog and sat on the toilet. I pulled open the plastic and held out a piece of meat for the animal squirming anxiously on my lap. He eagerly took it from my hand, then barked for more.

Mandy giggled, then leaned over to run some water in the tub, presenting me with a nice view of her ass.

I fed the dog a few more slices and received several licks on my chin for the effort.

"He's had enough," she said, taking the bag from my hand and securing the seal before setting it on the counter next to the sink.

The dog was prancing on my thighs and whimpering again. "He doesn't seem to think so."

"Maybe not, but you might change your mind if he decides to throw up all over you from eating too much, too fast."

I conceded that she made a good point. "Now what?" Mandy seemed to know what she was doing, so I decided to follow her lead.

"Now we see if we can get all that mud off him." She held out her hands for the dog, then lifted him in the air to expose his underbelly. "He's definitely a male." She turned him to show me his equipment. "We're going to have to come up with a name for you, aren't we, little guy?"

"Trouble" and "pain in the ass" were the names that popped into my head. I didn't believe Mandy would find them amusing, so I kept them to myself.

She cuddled the dog in her arms. "You aren't going to whine if I use some of your shampoo to clean him, are you?"

"No, but I will expect a payment for use of my supplies."

"What kind of payment are we talking about?" She innocently bit her lower lip, reminding me how soft and pliable it was, and how much I wanted to sample it some more.

"A kiss…or three will be sufficient."

"It sounds pretty steep, but I should be able to manage."

I relinquished my spot on the toilet and removed the dog from her arms. After shutting the door, I set him on the floor, then placed my hands on her hips and tugged her closer. "I would have said four, but I didn't want to push it." I leaned forward and captured her lips, taking my time, reveling in the soft texture before working my tongue into her mouth and boldly sampling.

When I pulled away, she breathlessly asked, "And the other two?"

"You can owe me, collection due at my leisure."

"Okay, then." She glanced at the dog. "Let's see about getting you cleaned up." She knelt next to the tub and set him in the water. "Do you have a plastic cup or something I can use to pour water over him to get the shampoo out?"

"Sure, I'll be right back." By the time I returned, the dog's fur was coated in a muddy lather and the water in the tub had changed to a murky brown.

While Mandy held the dog, I ran water into the plastic pitcher I'd found in the kitchen and poured it over his fur.

"Aren't you handsome now that the dirt is gone," she said, swiping her hand across the animal's back and wiping some of the excess water off his coat of sandy-blond, no longer a dark brown fur.

The dog slipped out of her grip, splashing and jumping, trying to get out of the water. For a little guy, he made a huge mess. Water ended up on the floor, on Mandy's face, and the front of her overalls and shirt were completely soaked. The animal clawed his way out of the tub, shaking and spraying more water the minute his paws touched the floor. She squealed and jumped to her feet, reaching for the dog and missing.

"No, you don't." I grabbed one of the towels and scooped him up before he could escape down the hall. Getting him dry was no easy feat. The little critter whimpered and squirmed, getting my shirt wet in the process.

Mandy took the other dry towel and used it to wipe her face and dab some of the moisture from her clothes. "That didn't go as well as I'd expected." She lifted the drain and rinsed out the tub, then draped the wet towels on the rim.

"Come on, you." She took the dog from my arms and headed to the living room. As soon as she set him on the floor, he walked over to the door, lifted one paw, and scratched.

"What is he doing?" I asked, baffled by the animal's behavior.

"He's telling us he needs to go outside." Mandy unlatched the screen, then pushed the door open and stepped onto the porch. "Maybe you won't have to worry about your floors after all." The dog slipped between her legs and ran straight to a nearby tree. A couple of sniffs later and he was lifting his leg. Once he'd completed his business, he scampered up the steps and back into the cabin.

Mandy smiled and turned her attention to me. "Would you mind if he stayed here?"

Was she crazy? "What? No... I..." Feeding and giving the animal a bath was one thing. Expecting me to take care of it was another. I had a hard enough time keeping myself out of trouble. What was I supposed to do with a dog? I stubbornly crossed my arms, ready to argue.

It was as if the dog understood what Mandy was asking. The little guy showed his support by dropping his rear end on the floor and swishing his tail back and forth. He stared up at me with expectant black eyes, then, to play on my sympathies, the damned thing threw in a few whimpers. I could've held out against the dog's persistent attempts to win me over. Mandy, not so much.

She moved closer to me and placed her hands on my arms. "Please. If I take him to the animal shelter, he'll end up getting put to sleep." She bit the side of her lip and glanced down at the dog. "I'd take him to my house, but I'm working all day. My dad can't take care of him, not with his broken leg."

I could feel my resolve wavering and narrowed my gaze, trying to hold strong against those pleading blue eyes.

"It would only be temporary, just until my dad recovers." She rubbed her fingers gently along my arm. "If it'll help keep him out of your way, I'll stop by every morning and take him with me while I work."

The warm glide of her skin against mine soothed the tension radiating through me but didn't alleviate the growing tightness in my pants. The prospect of having Mandy in my home every day had my wolf prancing. Keeping the dog, no matter how inconvenient, suddenly seemed appealing.

I lowered my arms and wrapped them around her waist, then pulled her against my chest. "I suppose I can deal with temporary." Yeah, I had plenty of experience with temporary. Permanent was still a struggle, but I was willing to work on it.

"Thank you." She smiled, placing her hands on my shoulders and giving me a kiss.

Never one to pass up an opportunity, I took control, turning what started out chaste into something passionate that left us panting. Since I wasn't ready to let her go, I pressed my forehead to hers and held her tight.

Once Mandy's breathing returned to normal, she said, "I should get back to work. That was a longer break than I normally take." She pulled out of my arms and headed for the door. "You two have fun. I'll see you in the morning."

I glanced at the dog, wondering how one small female had managed to turn my life upside down.

CHAPTER TEN

NICK

The furry critter was starting to grow on me, not that I'd admit it to Mandy. Having Bear around, the name I'd attached to the dog, hadn't been as bad as I'd imagined. He looked nothing like a bear. He was small, had stumpy legs, and his tail was longer than the entire length of his body. The name seemed to fit, and since the dog responded whenever I called him, I didn't bother to change it.

For the next few days, the three of us got into a routine. Every morning as promised, Mandy would stop by my home to pick up Bear before going to the next cabin in her schedule. And like most days, when she tried calling him to her truck, the dog would ignore her and make himself comfortable on my porch.

She'd even resorted to bringing him treats, and he still wouldn't budge. Bear didn't have a problem snatching the snacks out of her hand, then scurrying off to hide under the bench I'd placed on the porch in front of my living room window.

Today, the air was cool, and a mild breeze laced with

the scent of pine skimmed across my skin. After Mandy's visit shortly after sunrise, I'd headed to one of the other cabins and climbed onto the roof, intent on replacing the old and worn shingles. By early afternoon, the heat from the sun would be beating down on the roof, making it less bearable to work. I slid another shingle into place and picked up my hammer.

I enjoyed working with my hands and had ever since I'd worked on construction sites. Even if my grandfather hadn't left a portion of the resort to me, I'd still want to help my siblings, to feel useful. Handling some of the renovations was one of the ways I was contributing. It kept us from having to contract someone else to do it and saved us quite a bit of money.

"Nick."

I hadn't expected to see Mandy for a couple more hours and was surprised to hear her voice. "Yeah," I eagerly replied, then laid down the hammer and got to my feet. I walked to the edge of the roof and peered down at her. "Are you calling it quits already?" I smiled, something I found myself doing more and more since I'd met her.

She leveled her hand next to her forehead, shielding her eyes from the sun's glare. "No, I've run into some problems. I need to…"

I didn't give her time to finish before jumping from the roof's edge, landing two feet in front of her. Startled, she squeaked and fell backward. Damn, I hadn't meant to scare her. Luckily, I had enhanced reflexes and was able to stop her from falling by grabbing her hips and steadying her.

She gripped the front of my shirt. "You, you… I didn't know shifters could do that." She didn't pull away, seemingly too fascinated with my abilities to leap off a building without being hurt. "Is that how you got up there?"

I splayed my hands along her lower back, enjoying how good she felt pressed up against my chest. Lately, I couldn't get enough of her. There was a subtle hint of strawberry in her scent again, and it was driving my wolf crazy. I decided to keep her close a little longer. "Nah, I used the ladder." I glanced toward the side of the cabin where I'd braced the aluminum piece of equipment against the wall earlier. "Only cats can jump that high."

A grin tugged at the corners of Mandy's lips. She smoothed the fabric on my shoulders, then slid her hands around my neck. "You're not talking about house cats, are you?"

I winked. "Nope."

"Just how many kinds of shifters are there?"

"A few." I tightened my grip and nuzzled the side of her neck, nipping her earlobe. "So what did you need?" She'd mentioned running into a problem and I hoped it was something that required my assistance.

"Stop that. I have work to do." She squirmed, though her limited effort wasn't enough to get away from me. "I don't have all the parts I need to finish the repair on cabin 405. I tried to reach Reese to let him know, but he's not answering his phone. If you see him, would you tell him I had to drive over to the supply store in Hanford?"

Landlines worked fine in the area, but I knew there were times when cell phone coverage was intermittent. It might be the reason she was having trouble reaching my brother. Either that or he wasn't answering because he was tied up in interviews with candidates for the new security team. A task that was taking longer than expected. With the problems Bishop presented, Reese and Berkley had agreed to my idea of hiring more shifters versus using humans. If things turned ugly, they'd be better equipped to deal with Bishop's men.

Not many locals were willing to get involved with someone as powerful as Bishop, which limited our prospects to candidates from other cities or out-of-state— a time-consuming process.

Admittedly, I didn't want to let her go to Hanford by

herself. Not because she wasn't capable, but because I was finding it harder and harder to be away from her. My wolf was even worse, prancing around restlessly every minute she wasn't near us.

The only way I was going to calm my wolf and ease my own tension was to spend more time with her. "Why don't I go with you? I need to pick up some more shingles to finish the repair on the roof anyway."

Mandy furrowed her brows, her suspicious gaze landing on the stack of newly purchased shingles I'd placed on the end of the wooden porch. "Uh-huh."

"Let's take my truck." I spun her around, grasping her hand and tugging her toward the vehicle before she had a chance to tell me no.

I'd barely gotten her situated in the passenger seat when Bear barked and came running from his hiding spot underneath the porch. When we weren't at my cabin, the animal always found a place where he could burrow. I figured it was Bear's way of feeling protected, a safety mechanism he'd developed after being abandoned and having to take care of himself.

Bear's front paws reached the bottom of the doorframe, but his legs were too short to jump into the truck. I leaned forward and lent him some assistance by placing my hand under his rear and lifting.

Mandy tapped the seat in the middle. "Come on, boy." She smiled when Bear curled into a ball next to her, placing his head on her thigh.

Before heading to the main road, I made a quick stop at my cabin. "Sorry, boy. Not this time." I snatched Bear off the seat and carried him to the porch. "You're staying here." I wasn't too worried about Bear's comforts. He had the small cushioned bed Mandy had purchased for him, and I'd set a bowl of fresh water out earlier that morning so he wouldn't get thirsty before we returned.

Bear dropped his head on his front paws, doing his best to make me feel guilty. "Give me a break." I leaned closer and whispered, "I need some alone time with Mandy, okay?" When had I started explaining my actions to the dog? Since the scruffy creature had wormed its way into my heart and made himself at home, that's when. "I won't be gone long, I promise." I scratched Bear's head, then returned to the truck. I ignored his whimpers, knowing if I glanced over my shoulder, I'd end up changing my mind and taking the damned dog with us.

MANDY

After we dropped Bear off at Nick's cabin, I settled into my seat. I lowered the window, letting in the cool air that always carried a fresh hint of pine, to fill the cab's heated interior. I stared at the scenic landscape, admiring the hilly backdrop lined with walls of spruce trees and intermingled with tall ash. I'd made this drive countless times and never failed to be inspired by its astonishing beauty.

It didn't take a genius to know Nick didn't need more shingles to finish his roofing project. The proof was stacked on the edge of the porch. I wasn't sure why he'd insisted on driving me to Hanford, but I didn't argue when he helped me into his truck. Truth was I enjoyed spending time with him. I looked forward to our daily routine and found any excuse possible to be around him. I was in a constant state of awareness whenever I was near him. I'd been aroused from the moment he'd jumped off the roof and wrapped his arms around me.

Telling Nick I hadn't been able to reach Reese was the truth, sort of. I knew he wouldn't have a problem with me leaving, so I'd left a message on his voice mail. The trip to Hanford was going to take a couple of hours, and stopping by to see Nick and asking him to relay the message was the only excuse I could come up with to see him before I left.

Selfishly, I couldn't get enough of Nick and was thrilled

that he wanted to spend time with me. Part of me wanted to embrace the relationship, to throw caution to the wind, so to speak. Another part, the part that feared rejection and was afraid things would end badly, that one day I'd show up at his cabin and he'd be gone, fueled my reluctance. I didn't want to go through the same kind of heartache I'd suffered when Craig had cheated on me. Being cheated on and having someone leave weren't exactly the same thing, but enduring the pain and loneliness afterward would be no different.

I didn't understand why I was attracted to Nick's animalistic behavior and gruffness. It was so different from any of the men I'd ever dated, yet it appealed to me on so many levels. Even when he'd acted feral during our first encounter, I'd been drawn to him.

Contemplating thoughts about Nick had my gaze wandering in his direction. I couldn't help admiring his profile or the way the breeze gently teased the ends of his dark hair. There was a casual ease in the way he gripped the steering wheel and maneuvered the truck along the winding road. Living in the mountain wilderness suited him well, as if he'd been born to it and this was where he was meant to be. Berkley had voiced her opinion more than once about her concerns that he'd leave when his year ended. My friend wasn't the only one who hoped he'd make his stay permanent.

He'd warned me that he wasn't much of a conversationalist, yet his silence wasn't unsettling and didn't bother me. Being around Nick made me feel comfortable and safe.

Surprisingly, when I thought about it, I'd never felt this way when I was around Craig. Comfortable, maybe, but never like this. Not the rightness I felt with Nick, as if we should be together, as if I belonged with him and he belonged with me. "Huh." My pondering had me speaking out loud without meaning to.

"Did you say something?" Nick glanced at me

curiously, then returned his attention to the road.

Nothing I wanted to share. "No, just daydreaming."

He stretched his long arm in my direction, clasped my hand, and settled them on the seat between us. "About anything specific?"

You. "Work, my dad, the usual."

Nick frowned and squeezed my hand. "Is there a problem with your father? Because if there's anything you need…"

"No, he's fine. It's hard for him to spend all day at home doing pretty much nothing. I just worry he'll do something he shouldn't and make his leg worse."

His tight grip loosened a little. "Mandy, if you ever need anything, all you have to do is ask. You know that, right?"

"I appreciate your concern, but we're fine." I returned his squeeze when he shot me a skeptical look. "Really, we're good."

Nick slowed the vehicle as we reached the city limits. I dismissed the wave of disappointment when he released my hand to grip the wheel to make a turn.

"Have you been to Hanford before?" I asked when he made the next right turn onto the street leading directly to the store.

"A couple of times with Reese to talk to a contractor and some material suppliers." He pulled into the parking lot and stopped his truck in a spot three rows back from the entrance. He shifted sideways in his seat to face me. "The place is nice, but I like Ashbury better."

"Because it's smaller and the people are friendlier?" I asked, unsnapping my seat belt.

"You already know I don't do well with lots of people. Although, there is one person who holds my interest and for whom I'd gladly make an exception." The silver in his eyes darkened, and he raised his hand to my head, tucking some loose strands behind my ear.

I was mesmerized by his intense gaze and nervously

licked my lip. "And who would that be?" I hoped he was referring to me, but it didn't hurt to actually hear him confirm it.

"You already know." Nick caressed my cheek with his thumb, leaning closer toward me.

"Oh." I wasn't sure if the heat rushing across my skin was because we'd stopped and there was no longer air flowing in from outside or if his soft caresses were having an effect on me. A good guess said it was the latter.

Nick slid his hand along my neck and cupped the back of my head. He pressed his mouth to mine, gentle at first, then more possessive. This was different from the kisses we'd shared during our tasting game or other playful moments where Nick had made his interest known. The way he took control of the kiss had me moaning and left no doubts that he was staking a claim—on me.

I agreed with the idea, didn't I? I hadn't realized how much I'd grown to care about Nick in the few days I'd known him. I was falling for him in a big way, and it scared the hell out of me. A loud honking jolted my already racing heart and had us quickly pulling apart. I noticed a car had stopped a row over, and a fiftyish woman was leaning out the window, waving at a man who appeared to be around the same age and was pushing a cart across the lot.

"We should get going." I giggled nervously, then reached for the handle on my door.

Nick released a low growl and glared at the couple who'd interrupted us. "Fine," he grumbled and reluctantly exited the vehicle.

"Come on, grumpy." I took his hand and tugged him toward the store's entrance. "Hopefully, they'll have everything I need, and we can get you back home before you decide to eat someone."

"I'm not grumpy." Nick nudged my arm and shot me a petulant frown.

"You're worried I think you're a grouch, but snacking on someone doesn't bother you."

"Nope." He winked. "Is it supposed to?"

I grinned and shook my head. "Unbelievable." I paused in front of the sliding glass doors, waiting for them to open. Everything I needed was small, so once we were inside, I snatched a green plastic basket from the top of a stack near the door, then headed for an aisle toward the middle of the store. Even though I'd shopped here for years and knew where to find everything, I automatically glanced overhead at the rectangular white sign clearly stenciled with the word PLUMBING in bold black letters.

Without looking, I could feel Nick's eyes on me, studiously watching me pick through the different bins. "How did you learn so much about plumbing?"

I gave him a quick glance, then went back to examining the different parts. "My mom passed away when I was four. My dad couldn't afford daycare, so he took me along on his service calls."

I rummaged through another box of fittings until I found the part I needed. "As I got older, he let me help on the easier stuff. Eventually, I was able to do everything he could and started working some of the jobs by myself."

"Do you enjoy it?" Nick asked.

"Most of the time, I do. It's just…"

"What? I'd really like to know."

I stopped and gazed at the sincerity on his face. "I've always dreamed of being an interior designer. My backup would have been woodworking, but me and hammers…don't get along."

Nick placed his hand on my arm, the warmth comforting and arousing at the same time. "What's stopping you?"

"Money for one, time for another." I sighed. "When dad broke his leg, the doctors told him it would be a while before he could go back to work. It's not like we're rich or anything, and I knew if I didn't take care of his service calls, he'd try to do it himself."

"Isn't there anyone else who could help? Another

family member?" Nick asked.

"No, it's only the two of us. Luckily, I don't have to worry about him while I'm at work. Barb, the lady who lives next door, checks on him during the day. She's a widow, and to tell you the truth, I think she has a thing for my dad."

I dropped two more fittings into the basket. "I started some online courses, but between work and taking care of him, I don't have much time for myself. The other night at the bar was the first time I've been out in ages."

"Mandy?"

I grimaced when I recognized the familiar male voice. A voice that scratched along my skin and I'd prayed never to hear again. At first, I thought it was my imagination playing a cruel trick on me because I'd been thinking about him earlier. It wasn't until Craig spoke again that I finally acknowledged it was really him.

Heart hammering, I slowly turned and dismally watched Craig approach me, grinning as if we were the closest of friends. The same Craig who'd devastated my life and was the star in every nightmare I'd had for the past year. The closer he got, the more the pounding increased. Not because I was excited to see Craig, but because I'd never wanted to see or deal with him again.

After what happened with Adam, my current concern was Nick. I sensed his tension and glanced in his direction. Sure enough, his eyes had darkened and his hands were balled into tight fists. "Crap," I muttered to myself, wishing a hole would open in the floor and swallow Craig before he got any closer.

"Hey, Craig." I tried for polite but knew it was a wasted attempt by the sound of my voice. Craig stood a few inches shorter than six feet, had a slight paunch around his midsection and lacked the hard-muscled physique of the construction workers he supervised. I knew from when we'd dated that he spent his time reviewing plans, pushing paper and schmoozing owners, not getting any dirt under his nails or developing some calluses. Oh yeah, and how could I forget his personal pastime of screwing his assistants on the desk in his office trailer?

Craig presented me with a wide-toothed grin. "It's been a long time." He stopped a couple of feet in front of me, completely ignoring Nick when he spoke. "You look great." He slowly rolled his gaze over me, an appraising glimmer in his golden-brown eyes.

The scratchy itch was getting worse, and I wondered how I'd ever mistaken his leers for charm. I purposely made a big deal of tipping my head to the side and glancing behind him. "Where's Tisha?"

He furrowed his brows. "It's Trina, and she quit shortly after…you know."

Yeah, I knew all too well what he was implying. "Gee, I'm so sorry." I gripped the handle of my basket tighter. "From what I saw…" And I'd seen plenty. Images of their naked bodies entwined and sprawled across his desk were forever burned into my memory, and my father's. "She had a lot of promise." The sarcasm rolled off my tongue, and I smiled at my own humor.

"It was a mistake." Craig held out his hands apologetically. "One I deeply regret."

I highly doubted either of his admissions and almost snorted. After we'd broken up, I'd learned about several more of the "mistakes" he'd made when we were still together.

"Mandy." Nick's voice was deep, husky, laced with anger. "Aren't you going to introduce me to your *friend*?"

"I'm sorry. Nick, this is Craig, and he's not my friend." I wanted both men to be clear about Craig's status.

"How can you say that after all the time we spent together?" Craig formed a heavy pout with his lips. "What we meant to each other?"

"Do you really need an explanation?" I gritted my teeth so hard, I was sure I'd cracked a molar.

"Man, I've missed you. Why don't we take a walk

outside, catch up?" He paused for a moment. "Maybe talk about you giving me another chance to make things up to you?"

I couldn't believe the asshole was seriously asking me to forget what happened and take up where we left off. Before I had a chance to tell Craig what he could do with his invitation, Nick was growling and in his face. "In case you hadn't noticed, Mandy is with me, and I don't appreciate anyone messing with what's mine."

Okay, the "mine" thing was new. I knew we were slowly moving in the direction of developing something I would consider special, but Nick's admission totally blindsided me. I didn't have time to consider what he'd said before movement to the right caught my attention, and I noticed several other customers hovering closer, eavesdropping on our conversation. Great, the last thing I needed was for Nick to wolf out and frighten the locals.

"Nick." I ran my hand along the tightly bunched muscles on his arm, hoping to distract him. "He's *so* not worth it."

NICK

It wasn't hard to determine from Mandy's conversation with Craig that she'd been in some sort of relationship with him, and it wasn't sitting well with my wolf or me. I wasn't naive enough to believe that someone as gorgeous as her had never been involved with anyone before I'd met her. It didn't mean I was happy about meeting the male or would tolerate his interference.

Whatever their past history had been, it was clearly not something she wanted any part of now. She was doing her best to hide her uneasiness, but I wasn't fooled in the slightest. I'd recognized her discomfort in the sarcastic tone of her voice, the way she nervously bit her lower lip, and the numerous glances in my direction.

The male's presence was upsetting her and aggravating me. I didn't appreciate the way Craig's lustful gaze continually skimmed over every inch of her as if she were a scrumptious meal and his for the taking. She wasn't Craig's, she was mine. My mate. I planned to make sure Craig understood what that meant even if I had to draw his blood to do it.

"Nick." Mandy's soothing voice drew me from my murderous thoughts. "He's *so* not worth it." It was growing increasingly hard to control my wolf. The vehemence she directed at Craig was the only thing keeping me from letting my animal surface and rip the male apart.

I didn't think she'd appreciate the efforts I would take to protect her, so the sooner I got Mandy away from him, the better. "Do you have everything you need?" I kept my hardened gaze locked on Craig and his determined glare.

She glanced at the basket on her arm, taking inventory of the few items inside. "Yeah, this will do it."

"Good, then we should go." I urged Mandy in the direction of the checkout registers. With her attention focused elsewhere, I allowed my wolf's anger to emerge in my eyes and glared at Craig. "Mandy is no longer your concern, so stay the hell away from her."

His face paled to an ashy hue. He stumbled backward. "What the…" he mumbled, his remaining words incoherent.

"Are we clear?" I asked, wanting to make sure the man never bothered Mandy ever again.

Craig bobbed his head, made a choking noise, and appeared as if he was going to urinate in his pants. I glanced at the man's crotch and was disappointed to see that the fabric was still dry.

Satisfied he'd gotten the message, I quickly caught up with Mandy in the short line by the nearest cash register. "Are you okay?" I placed my hand protectively along her lower back.

"Fine."

I could tell by the way her muscles tensed under my hand that she was still upset. She didn't say anything during the remainder of our time in the store, not uttering another word even after she got into my truck and snapped her belt into place.

Did her silence mean she still had feelings for Craig? Had she decided I wasn't worth her efforts? I hated that years of rejection had me struggling with self-doubt. I gripped the steering wheel and focused on her.

"I take it you and Craig have a history." She was my mate, the only woman I wanted, and I didn't want to lose her. Her being human made things more complicated. She was aware my kind existed, but I didn't know if she was capable of feeling our bond. If she was a shifter, she'd understand our connection and I'd have already claimed her.

I would never force her to accept me and had planned to take my time gaining her trust and winning her heart. I couldn't do either if she was involved with someone else.

"Yes." Mandy had been staring at her lap and raised her head to meet my gaze. "It ended a long time ago."

"Do you still care about him?" It was the hardest question I'd ever had to ask anyone. I held my breath, hoping and praying I hadn't misread the situation.

"No." She shook her head.

It was all I needed to hear. The tightness in my chest abated, and I relaxed my grip on the wheel. From what she'd said to Craig in the store and the worry still creasing her brow, I was certain there was more to the story. I eased her hand into mine. "Do you want to talk about it?" I was surprised to hear the words come out of my mouth.

Even more surprising was Mandy's huge grin and the patronizing way she patted my hand. "And you said you weren't good with people."

I groaned, silently cursing Berkley for wearing off on me with her "you need to learn to communicate" speeches.

CHAPTER ELEVEN

NICK

Now that I had Mandy all to myself, I wasn't ready to end my time with her by returning to my cabin. On a whim, I turned off the main highway onto a dirt road, and in minutes, the truck was surrounded by trees. The surface was worn, and the areas that rarely saw sunlight were gouged with deep, muddy ruts pooled with water from a recent rain storm.

My Ford pickup was a newer model, had four-wheel drive, and, if required, could handle the deteriorated condition of the road without any problems.

Mandy had dozed during our drive, and after the first bump bounced her awake, she glanced out the window, then back at me. "Uh, Nick?"

"Yeah."

"Where are we going?" She didn't sound alarmed, only curious.

"Shortcut back to my place," I said innocently, leaving out the part where I planned to stop somewhere else first. In the short time I'd been living at the resort, I'd explored a majority of the area. I'd discovered this road by accident when I'd been out running as my wolf. If we continued on this route, we'd return to the resort...eventually.

"This is not a shortcut. It's one of the access roads to the falls. It's going to take at least another hour to get back to your cabin." Mandy braced one hand on the seat, the other on the door to keep from being jostled. "Reese is going to be upset, and you're going to get me fired." She groaned and glared at me. "You do remember me telling you about needing the money, right?"

"I'm one of the partners, remember?" At first, I hadn't wanted the position and had reluctantly stepped into the role with a lot of coercing from Reese and Berkley. If being in charge allowed me more time with Mandy, I planned to use it to my advantage. "Since you're with me, I'd say your job is safe."

She wrinkled her brow, still unconvinced. "So you're going to protect me when Reese has a fit because the deadlines aren't being met?"

"Absolutely." An afternoon alone with her was worth any lecture I'd get from my brother. "You have my word." She was cute when she was mad, and I wanted to kiss the frown from her face.

"I'm holding you to that." She returned her attention to our surroundings.

Five minutes later, the road curved, and the thinning trees presented us with a glimpse of the falls. Mandy glanced at me, suspicion narrowing her gaze. "You're not going back to the resort, are you?"

"Not right away." I drove the truck onto a semi-level area that had been cleared and covered with gravel, providing an overlook for the massive display. A two-foot guardrail constructed out of tree trunks ran along the edge to prevent anyone from driving their vehicle over the steep ledge.

A tall mountain wall covered in rock, trees, and underbrush rose up in front of us. Numerous streams of clear water cascaded over smooth layers of black and gray boulders, then splashed into a large pool of crystal green water below. Seneca Falls had become one of my favorite spots in the mountain wilderness. Not only was the view spectacular, but the water was derived from a hot spring, and swimming wasn't prohibited.

"Is there a reason you decided to bring me here?"

"Berkley is always telling me I need to lighten up and learn how to have fun." For once, I planned to take my sister's advice.

"So that's what we're doing, having fun?" she asked suspiciously.

"Yep. Come on." As soon as I opened the door, a layer of cool, moist air covered my skin, and I was greeted by the rumble of water beating and splashing its way to the awaiting pool below. I walked around to Mandy's side of the vehicle, then took her hand and tugged her toward one of numerous paths that would get us closer to the falls.

The walkway was narrow and steep in several places. Maneuvering wasn't a problem for me, but Mandy struggled, slipping in the loose dirt and clutching my arm to keep from falling. "Would you like me to carry you?"

"And have us both end up on the ground? No, thanks." Her amused grin told me she'd considered it before turning me down.

"Suit yourself." I continued moving forward, enjoying the warmth from her hands and having her fingertips dig into my skin every time she lost her footing.

Eventually, the ground leveled out, and instead of stopping to observe the largest cluster of flowing water, I continued walking. "This way." I led her into a narrow space between two large trees and onto a path I knew wasn't visible from the area we'd left. The trail curved to the right and ended up near a smaller pool in a more secluded area.

"This is beautiful." Mandy gaped at the landscape. "I've been out here quite a few times and never knew this was here." She glanced back at him. "How did you find it?"

"I like to explore when I'm out on a run."

"You mean when you do your wolfy thing?"

"Yeah, when I do my wolfy thing." If anyone else had made the comment, I'd have taken offense, assuming it was meant as a dig because of the wild side of my nature. Coming from Mandy, it was adorable, and I laughed. She wasn't being mean; she was simply stating a fact.

"Do you suppose you could show me your wolf sometime?"

I pulled her into my arms and pressed a kiss to her lips. "Anything for you." The idea pleased and enticed me. My wolf strutted, ready to show off for his mate. Our mate.

I perked my ears, listening to the neighboring sounds and ensuring there was no one around to witness my shift. I kicked off my shoes, then tugged my shirt over my head before tossing it on the ground.

MANDY

"Whoa, what are you doing?" I couldn't believe Nick was stripping in front of me. Even though I'd gotten a glimpse of his torso the first day we'd met, I couldn't stop staring at his chest. Seeing those contoured abs and pectorals in a darkened hallway versus the bright sunshine were two different things. His skin was a road map of fine lines and a rich, golden tan. After having more time to scrutinize, I decided his bare chest was very impressive.

Nick's hand hovered over the button on his jeans. "Did you change your mind about seeing my wolf?" He raised his brows daringly.

"No, I…" I hadn't considered the possibility he'd need to take off his clothes when I'd asked him to shift, and it was too late to change my mind now.

"My clothes will be shredded, and this is all I have to wear, unless you'd prefer I drive you back to my cabin naked."

104

My mind flooded with all kinds of images. Images that had heat scorching a path across my skin, all the way to my toes. He was only shifting, right? Was it wrong of me to ogle his gorgeous physique before he transformed into his wolf? I clamped my lips together, unwilling to share my thoughts. Nick seemed to have read my mind, because he chuckled and unzipped his jeans.

He made quick work of removing the rest of his clothes. He was a big guy, and his dimensions extended to the large, stiff cock jutting between his legs. He was turned on and, judging by his huge grin, was proud of it. "Ready?"

Ready for what? I was too busy drooling to comprehend that he was talking about his wolf and not the direction my thoughts were taking me. And believe me, my thoughts involved my mouth, hands, and a lot of touching.

"Mandy?" He tipped his head, asking my permission to continue.

Since I was on sensation overload and unable to speak, I nodded.

One second, Nick was standing there, and before I could blink, a huge black wolf, bigger than any I'd ever seen, was stalking toward me. The hungry way his wolf was staring at me was a little unnerving. I had to remind myself that Nick, the man, was behind that predatory gaze.

He brushed along the front of my legs and nuzzled my palm with his snout. "Nick, your wolf is beautiful." I sank my fingers into his fur. It was thicker and coarser than his human hair, but no less tempting to play with. He pressed against my legs and growled, a low rumble that vibrated beneath my fingertips.

"Like that, do you?" I continued massaging his back, working my way to his rump.

Once I stopped, he turned so he was facing me, then nudged my stomach hard enough to make me take a few steps backward and closer to the water's edge. "Stop it." I knew Nick would never hurt me and pushed his head aside. The persistent creature ignored me, caught the hem of my shorts with his teeth, and tugged. Was he trying to get me to take my clothes off? "No."

The next thing I knew, the wolf was gone and Nick was standing in front of me. "Swim with me…teach me how to have fun."

He pulled me into his arms, gently following up his plea with a nip to my neck. "Unless you're afraid…" He let the challenge hang in the air.

"It's not the water I have a problem with." I'd been swimming in the springs plenty of times when I was a teenager. Of course, I'd been wearing a swimsuit and been with a bunch of girls. I'd never been in the water naked with a full-grown man and never with one so handsome, he made my mouth water.

"Oh no," he whispered, grazing my skin with his teeth. "What is it, then?"

"The devious antics of a big bad wolf." I groaned and exposed more of my throat to his mouth.

"What if I promised to keep my *hands* to myself?" He swiped his tongue across my skin. "You'll have to beg me to touch you." He took a step back, releasing me completely.

If I were being honest, I wanted him touching me all over and couldn't help feeling a little disappointed that he'd stopped. I wasn't usually so daring, but I was convinced I would win and decided to take him up on his tempting challenge. "Then I should be safe, because I have no intention of begging."

"Really?" Nick quirked a brow, and I knew he'd taken the bait.

"Uh-huh." I slowly unhooked the clasps on my overalls. The bib and straps dangled from my waist, exposing the crop top I wore underneath. Nick moaned, his gaze lowering to the bare skin along my midsection. I couldn't help notice he was hard again when I poised my fingers over the button on the right side of my shorts. "You need to turn around."

"What?" He snapped his attention back to my face. "Why?"

"No hands, no peeking, no temptation," I taunted.

"So unfair," he grumbled and slowly turned to face away from me.

I sat on a nearby rock, then untied and slipped out of my boots and socks. After stripping out of my overalls and shirt, I contemplated removing my black panties and bra and decided against it. I was glad I'd taken the time to select a matching set when I glanced in Nick's direction and caught him staring at me over his shoulder. "What happened to no peeking?"

"What happened to going naked?" he countered, giving me one of his lopsided grins.

"I don't recall you saying anything about skinny-dipping." I shook my head and walked toward the water, careful to avoid any sharp rocks. Once the water reached my hips, I turned just in time to see Nick climb onto a large boulder and dive into the deeper part of the pool.

"Show-off," I said as soon as his head breached the water's surface.

"Couldn't resist…" He smiled and swiped the wet hair back from his face. "Now, about that begging." He stalked toward me, sending miniature waves rippling across the transparent surface. A glimmer of desire shimmered in the depths of his gray eyes, and once again, I was reminded of his predatory side.

Anticipation raced through my system, and I moved backward, never letting my gaze leave his. I hadn't realized he'd maneuvered me into a shallow alcove until my back pressed into a smooth rock wall. He stopped several inches in front of me, then leaned in close. Close enough for me to feel the heat coming off his body without our skin touching. Close enough to have my nipples pebbling and a warm, needy ache building in my core.

He sniffed the air and smirked, knowing exactly what kind of effect he was having on me and enjoying it immensely. He brushed his lips across my mouth—feather-light, teasing, short.

I swallowed a moan. My heart raced, and I was finding it hard to breathe. "What happened to no touching?"

He pressed another kiss to my jaw. "I promised to keep my hands to myself. I didn't say anything about my mouth."

Nick placed his hands on the rock near my shoulders. "Didn't anyone ever tell you it's never a good idea to tempt a wolf, especially a wild one?" He pressed his lips to the skin along my throat, reaching the base and nipping the skin near my collarbone.

"I must have missed that lesson." I gasped, barely able to keep my hands pressed against my thighs, my resolve to keep from begging slowly dwindling.

The water where we were standing wasn't deep and left my scantily covered breasts exposed. A fact Nick wasted no time using to his advantage. Lowering his head, he used his teeth to push aside the flimsy lace. He latched on to my nipple and sucked it into his mouth, then teased the tip by circling it with his tongue.

I shuddered and arched my back, no longer able to fight the pleasurable sensations racking my body. I gripped the underside of his arms and moaned. "Please, Nick."

"Please what?" He licked the side of my breast, then peeled back the lace on the other one.

"Touch me," I whimpered.

NICK

Mandy's plea to continue had me wanting her in the worst way. What started out as playful teasing had my cock throbbing to be inside her. I wanted our first time to be somewhere private where there wasn't a possibility we'd be interrupted and had no intention of taking her here. It didn't mean I couldn't play some more and ensure she reached her climax.

I pulled her into my arms, sliding my hands down her back to cup her ass and grind her against my erection. I sucked her other nipple into my mouth and twirled my tongue over the tip, smiling against her skin when she moaned and dug her nails into my shoulders.

I kissed my way along her chest, stopping to graze the skin at the base of her neck with my teeth. Someday, if I were to claim her, this would be where I placed my mark. My wolf was in total agreement and forced a growl to rumble in my chest.

Mandy dropped her head back giving me better access to her neck. I pressed kisses along salty-sweet skin, tasting the lobe of her ear. "Mandy."

"Mmm."

"Spread your legs for me." I nipped her skin, gripping her ass tighter and lifting.

She wrapped her legs around my waist, making pleasurable moans when her core rubbed against my hard shaft. Holding back, restraining myself from taking what I truly wanted was exquisite torture. This was about her pleasure, and I longed to watch her come apart in my arms.

Working my fingers along the edge of her panties, I slid my hand inside the silky fabric, gliding across her wet curls, then slipping two fingers inside her dampened folds. She was more than ready to take me, and again I fought the urge to thrust my cock inside her.

I pushed in and out of her slowly, building a steady rhythm while I continued to taste and tease her throat.

"Yes." She arched her back, pushing harder against my hand.

She was close. I could tell by the way she clenched around my fingers. I continued to thrust, increasing the pace. When I pressed my thumb to her clit, she bucked against my hand and moaned. I pressed my mouth over hers, capturing her scream as she shuddered through her orgasm. I continued pumping, drawing out her pleasure until her grip on my shoulders slackened and she slumped against my chest.

I started to worry when Mandy didn't move even after her breathing had returned to normal. "Mandy?"

"Huh."

"How are you doing?"

"I… There are no words." She lifted her head and smiled. "Berkley was wrong when she said you don't know how to have fun."

I grinned and kissed her forehead. "I should get you back." Loosening my grip, I waited until she was standing on her own, then took her hand and led her out of the water.

Once we reached the area where we'd left our clothes, Mandy grabbed the end of her braid and squeezed out the excess moisture.

"Here, wear this." I handed her my shirt. "We'll throw your wet things in the dryer when we get back to my cabin."

"Thanks."

I quickly tugged on my pants and shoes while she pulled the shirt over her head. The oversized garment almost touched her knees, making it easy for her to reach underneath and remove her soaked bra and panties.

I grabbed the rest of her belongings, placed them in her hands, then carefully scooped her into my arms. "What are you doing?"

"Protecting that gorgeous ass of yours from landing in the dirt."

She clutched her clothes in one arm and wrapped the other around my neck. "And who's going to protect your sexy backside if you trip and fall?"

"I'm a wolf. Falling is not in our nature."

What I'd failed to tell Mandy when I'd suggested we get back was that I had no intention of letting her return to work right away. After parking the truck in front of my cabin, I walked around and opened her door.

She'd put her boots and socks on during the drive, so I didn't have an excuse to carry her inside.

"Thanks for driving me to Hanford." She grabbed her clothes and the plastic bag of supplies off the seat, then hopped out of the truck.

As soon as we reached the porch, Bear lazily climbed out from under the bench, then happily swished his tail. "Hey, there, did you miss us?" Mandy scratched behind his ears, then headed inside.

She stopped near the kitchen and held up her wet underwear. "Where's the dryer? If it's all right with you, I'll toss these inside and pick them up on my way home."

"We'll worry about these later." I took everything she was holding and plopped it on the counter. I pulled her into my arms and hoisted her over my shoulder.

"Nick, what the heck…" she squealed and pressed her hands against my bare back.

"We're not done having fun yet." I stepped into the kitchen. Being the adoring sister that she was, Berkley thought it would be cute to give me a box a condoms for a housewarming gift. At the time, I wasn't amused and had absently tossed them into a drawer.

"We're not?" she asked curiously with a hint of enthusiasm.

"No." I grabbed the box, then headed for the bedroom. "Besides, you still owe me two kisses, and I plan to collect."

MANDY

I had to admit Nick's naughty caveman antics were kind of a turn-on. I was still sensitive from the epic orgasm he'd given me during our time in the pool, and it didn't take much for me to be aroused again. I hated to think what Reese would do if he stopped by the other cabin and didn't find me. "Nick, I really should get back to work."

"Later." He continued down the hallway to the bedroom, shutting the door before Bear could follow us inside. I got a glimpse of the small black-and-gold box he placed on the nightstand before hauling me off his shoulder and tossing me onto the middle of the bed.

I bounced and giggled, propping on my elbows and striving for a serious expression and failing. "Your brother is going to kill me."

"Like I said, perks to being the boss." He reached for one of my ankles, then the other, quickly removing and tossing my boots and socks on the floor.

"The shirt needs to go." He fingered the waistband on his pants, expectantly waiting for me to do as he'd asked.

"You do know you're very demanding to work for, don't you?" I sat up and reached for the hem of the shirt.

"Maybe so, but I know what I want." Down went the zipper. "And right now, I want you."

His irises darkened to a gunmetal gray, letting me know his wolf wanted me too. By the time I'd pulled off the shirt, he was standing at the foot of the bed naked, wearing a huge grin. I lowered my gaze, taking in his trim hips and thick, hard shaft, then licked my lower lip, quivering and wet with need. I wasn't interested in foreplay, I wanted him, and I wanted him now. I leaned back, knees bent, and legs spread. "Then what are you waiting for?"

The bed dipped from his weight as he crawled—more like stalked—toward me, reminding me once again that he wasn't completely human. He knelt between my legs and reached for the box on the nightstand. After removing a condom and rolling it down his shaft, he settled his hips between my thighs.

"You are so beautiful." Nick cupped the side of my face, then placed his mouth over mine. With a swipe of his tongue, our slow, sensuous kiss became more demanding, more possessive. I eagerly opened my mouth, submitting to his dominance. I was panting when he moved his attentions to my breast.

He was doing amazing things to my nipple with his tongue, the sensation tugging at my core. I released a soft cry and tangled my fingers in his hair, urging him to continue.

When he slipped his hand between my legs and rubbed his thumb over my sensitive flesh, I bucked, nearly coming off the bed. I ached to have him inside me. "Please, Nick. I want you…"

He groaned and released my breast, then shifted his weight and entered me with a careful thrust. The fit was tight, perfect, and intensely pleasurable.

Nick pushed in and out of me, hitting all the right places. I slid my hands down his back, felt the muscles ripple beneath my touch. I was already close to an orgasm, and when I finally reached it, I knew it was going to be a strong one. He must have sensed it as well, because his movements became faster and harder. I wrapped my legs across the back of his thighs, arching to meet his powerful thrusts. I reached the pinnacle, crying his name, shuddering and hurtling over the edge.

Nick growled, giving me a final thrust and finding his own release. He collapsed, using his elbows to keep most of his weight off me. When his breathing evened out, he nuzzled the side of my neck. "I kinda like this having-fun thing." He nipped my earlobe. "Maybe we should practice some more to make sure I'm doing it correctly."

I trembled with anticipation, then groaned. Partner or not, the man was going to get me fired.

CHAPTER TWELVE

NICK

I was going to kill Reese if he was the one pounding on the door and ruining my perfect moment with Mandy. Other than my brother and sister, she was the only one who visited my cabin. Since she was curled up next to me in my bed, I could eliminate her from the list. The cell phone in the pocket of my discarded pants had rung with Reese's familiar tone at least three times in the last five minutes, leading me to believe it was him.

It was the second afternoon this week that I'd been able to coax Mandy to stop work early and spend some time in my bed. Judging by the amount of light filtering through the blind on the window, it was midafternoon and we hadn't been napping long. "Mandy." I brushed some loose curls off her face, loving the soft noise she made. "We need to get up. Someone's at the door."

"Crap." She must have finally heard the banging, because she widened her eyes. "Who do you think it is?"

"It's probably Reese. He's been calling." Panic blossomed on her face, and I immediately wished I hadn't said anything. Tension and the overwhelming need to protect her pulsed from my wolf, letting me know he wasn't happy about it either. I remembered Mandy's voiced concerns about losing her job and wanted to reassure her. "Hey, don't worry."

"But…"

"I told you everything will be okay." I pressed a kiss to her forehead. "We don't have anything to hide, and we'll deal with it together."

"Okay." She rolled from my arms and off the bed, then reached for her clothes.

Another bang on the door had me doing the same. I tugged on my pants and grabbed my shirt on the way out of the room.

"You better have a damned good reason for bothering me," I grumbled and pulled the shirt over my head. I yanked the door open and stared through the screen in surprise at the stranger standing on my porch. He was an older man, early fifties maybe, with sandy-brown hair and blue eyes a shade darker than Mandy's. He was dressed in khaki shorts and a short-sleeved cotton shirt with an orange-and-yellow patterned print. If it wasn't for the bulky black ankle boot protecting some type of injury, I'd have thought he was headed for a Hawaiian vacation.

"I didn't mean to bother you." The man smiled brightly, forming dimples. "I was told up at the lodge that I might find my daughter here."

"Your daughter?" It took me a moment to realize why his features seemed oddly familiar. He was Roy Jenson, Mandy's father. Before I had a chance to say anything, Mandy was at my side, smoothing her mussed hair.

One glance at our visitor and the color drained from her face. "D-Dad," she stammered. "What are you doing here?"

"I tried calling, but you weren't answering your phone." Roy glanced at me, taking a longer look this time, giving me a thorough perusal. Not that I blamed him. The man had found me with his daughter, and it didn't take a lot of intelligence to figure out what we'd been doing. I wasn't ashamed of being caught and, if given the choice, would take her to my bed all over again. I was more concerned about Mandy's reaction. Would she think I was good enough to acknowledge, or would she pretend our close connection didn't exist?

I swallowed back the lump of rejection building in my throat and glanced at Mandy, unsure how to proceed.

"Do you suppose I could come in?" Roy asked.

"Sure." I pushed open the screen for him, glad he was still smiling. Bear had remained under the bench the whole time and finally decided to make his presence known. He scurried inside with Roy slowly limping behind him.

I turned and glared at Bear, who'd found a spot near my feet and was happily sitting on his rear and swishing his tail. "Some guard dog you are."

"Hey, there, boy." Roy gripped the arm of the nearby sofa and bent forward to scratch the dog's head. "You must be the little guy Mandy told me about." Once he was standing again, Roy directed his attention at his daughter. "Aren't you going to introduce us?"

"I'm sorry." Mandy gave her father a quick hug, then returned to my side. "Dad, this is Nick. He's Berkley's brother."

Roy held out his hand. "It's nice to finally meet you. My girl here speaks rather highly of you."

"She does?" I was surprised and exhilarated by the news.

Roy nodded, giving me another one of his perusals. "I see why she likes you."

"Dad," Mandy interrupted, her warning insistent. "What happened to your cast?"

"The doc took it off, says it's healing nicely."

"Did he give you permission to drive with that thing on your foot?" She pointed at the cumbersome boot.

"I didn't drive." Roy glanced through the screen at the metallic silver car parked on the graveled drive next to my truck. "Barb brought me."

"That still doesn't explain why you're here." Mandy gave her father an admonishing look.

"Oh, right. As you already know, I've been going a little stir-crazy. When Barb mentioned that she'd never been up here, I suggested we make the trip." Roy grinned more at me than at his daughter. "I was curious to see what you've been doing." He held up his hand. "Before you go getting all suspicious about your old man's motives, I had another reason for coming out here."

"Yeah, and what would that be?" Mandy slapped her hands on her hips.

"Remember the order you placed for the replacement vanity?"

"Yes, why?" she asked.

"The company delivered it to the house. The driver was a young kid, and he seemed confused when I told him how to get here. I thought it would be easier to bring it out here myself. This way, I get to spend some extra time with you and get to know Nick a little better." Roy glanced at me and winked. "Mind if I take a look around?"

"Help yourself." I waved toward the living room, stepping aside so Roy could hobble past me.

Mandy gave me an apologetic smile and mouthed the word *sorry*. I pressed a kiss to her forehead, letting her know I was okay with her father's visit.

Roy's attention immediately went to the table I'd handcrafted. He glanced at me over his shoulder. "Mandy said you were talented, but this..." He ran his hand across the wooden surface. "This is amazing work. Do you ever sell anything you make?"

"No, I've never considered it." I'd started the hobby to relieve stress, not to supplement my income.

"Well, if you ever do, let me know." Roy scratched his chin. "There are quite a few people in the area who'd be interested."

"I will, thanks."

Roy gave me a brief nod, then turned to Mandy. "Why don't you show me what you've been working on?"

"This way." She released my hand and led her father down the hall. I was glad the bedroom was at the opposite end of the cabin and Roy wouldn't be able to see the rumpled state of my bed. It wouldn't bother me, but I had a feeling it would upset Mandy.

Once Roy had inspected the plumbing underneath the sink and given her a proud-fatherly compliment, we headed out to the car so I could unload the new vanity. Shortly after introducing me to Barb, her sister called with an emergency, putting an end to their outing.

"I guess we'll be going, then." Roy's disappointment over having to leave was evident in the way he dropped his head and slumped his shoulders.

Surprisingly, I was enjoying the older man's company and wanted to spend more time with him. "Why don't you and Mandy stay, have dinner with us up at the lodge?"

"Are you sure? I don't want to impose," Roy replied enthusiastically, already moving away from Barb's car.

"Berkley's been experimenting with new dishes for the restaurant and will be thrilled to have more people to do some taste testing."

"I have to admit, I wouldn't mind not having to cook when I get home," Mandy offered.

Roy wrung his hands in anticipation. "Well then, it sounds like we'll be staying."

MANDY

After my father practically invaded Nick's home, an invitation to dinner was the last thing I'd expected. Once we arrived at the lodge and my father was headed toward the kitchen, I pulled Nick aside. I'd been thinking about our afternoons together, his challenging dares, his playful kisses, and the way he'd manipulated my body into passionate pleasure.

I was worried Nick might be feeling guilty about what had happened between us, especially after the way he'd met my father. It was bad enough that my father had shown up at Nick's cabin unannounced. What would have happened if he'd caught us together in his bed? "I'm really sorry about my dad. You didn't need to ask us to stay." I lowered my gaze, afraid of having my fears confirmed. "I know you like your privacy and…"

"I wanted to do this." Nick touched my chin, gently lifting it until our gazes met. "Mandy, you're important to me. You're my…" He paused to ponder his words. "What I mean is, I don't scare easily. Roy seems like a great guy, and I'd like to get to know him better, unless you'd rather I didn't."

Relieved, I smiled. "Don't be silly. If you're comfortable with having him around, then it's okay with me."

"Good." He grabbed my hand. "Let's go. I had quite a workout this afternoon, and I'm starving."

I groaned and let him lead me down the hall. I knew he was referring to our lovemaking session and didn't need a mirror to see the bright red blossoming on my cheeks. Again. I wondered if Nick would ever grow tired of purposely making me blush.

Nick had called ahead to let Berkley know he was bringing guests. When we entered in the dining area of the restaurant, she was already placing bowls and platters of food on one of the long rectangular tables.

She glanced in our direction, her gaze landing on our joined hands, and smiled. "Hey, guys, I hope you all like Italian." She grabbed two bottles of Merlot, setting one on each end of the table. Next, she pulled back the foil on a pan of lasagna and placed it next to a large lettuce salad topped with olives, tomato slices, and croutons. She'd even draped a cloth napkin in a basket and filled it with freshly baked breadsticks.

"This looks great, sweetie." My father gave Berkley a hug and kissed her on the cheek. "I've missed your visits."

"Don't you mean you've missed my cooking?" Berkley teased.

"Well, that too." He shuffled to sit on a chair near the end where he could stretch out his booted foot.

"Come on, everyone, take a seat." When Berkley began cutting squares in the large pan of lasagna, everyone in the room moaned at the delicious smell. It didn't take long for everybody to get settled and begin passing the food around.

The conversation throughout the meal remained light, everyone too busy enjoying the meal. After finishing two helpings of everything, Reese pushed his plate aside and leaned back in his chair. "Roy, what do you know about Desmond Bishop?"

My father frowned, his expression sobering. "That man's a nasty piece of work. Why?" He took a swallow of his wine. "You weren't considering doing business with him, were you?"

"No, but we've been having some problems." Reese went on to explain about our recent break-ins and Bishop's offer to purchase the resort.

"From what I've heard, he has the Hanford police in his pocket, so you won't get any help there." My father reached for his third breadstick.

"I figured as much, which is why we've hired a security team to keep an eye on things."

"You need to be careful. He's dangerous and has run a couple other companies out of business to get what he wants." He cast a nervous glance in my direction. "Should I be worried about my daughter's safety?"

"I've got one of my guys checking on her throughout the day."

That explained why I'd seen Bryson drive by the cabin where I was working a few times every day. Berkley had seemed overly anxious when she'd told me about the damage to the cabin, but I'd assumed it was stress related to opening the resort. I should have known she was trying to protect me. She'd taken on the role from the time we were teens.

I glanced at Reese, who was speculatively staring at the table and rubbing his chin. I'd seen that faraway look before, and uneasiness settled over me.

Finally, he returned his gaze to my father. "Maybe it would be a good idea to have someone else complete the rest of the cabins. I'll see if I can bring in a contractor from Denver to finish."

"No," I snapped. "You hired us...me to do this job, and I plan to see it through to the end. I'm not about to leave you shorthanded, and I won't let Desmond Bishop or anyone else dictate where I work."

"Mandy, I think you should listen..."

I cut my father off by holding up my hand and giving Reese and him one of my don't-bother glares.

"I'll make sure nothing happens to her." Nick draped his arm across the back of my chair and protectively gripped my shoulder.

Having him close with his warm hand pressed against my skin always made me feel safe. Heck, being with him anytime anywhere always felt right. "Hey, I'm not completely helpless," I chided and patted his thigh. "I have some pretty good wrench-wielding ninja skills."

Nick chuckled. "I'll bet you do." He nuzzled the side of my neck and whispered in my ear. "I'd love to see them the next time we're alone."

CHAPTER THIRTEEN

NICK

Today was the day. My wolf and I were both laden with anxiety, the animal because he would finally get what he wanted, and me because I feared I might lose the one thing that meant the most to me.

Mandy.

I maneuvered my truck along the gravel road and nervously fingered the rim of the clear plastic container sitting on the seat next to me. Inside was a batch of Berkley's double-fudge brownies, which I'd had her prepare specifically for this occasion.

Bear was curled up on the passenger seat. He sniffed the container, his cold nose brushing against my hand. "These are not for you." I gave him a warning scowl.

After taking one more sniff, Bear made a disgruntled noise and laid his head on his paws. The animal was more devious than my wolf. He pretended to be disinterested, but I knew better. Out of my peripheral vision, I caught him opening one eye and focusing it on the contents hidden inside.

I'd come to realize a few things over the last few days.

The resort was my home, my permanent home, complete with a brother and sister. It didn't matter that we missed out on a childhood together and were still learning how to coexist. They'd unconditionally welcomed me into their lives and made me a part of their family, and I had no intention of giving them up.

I'd embraced the knowledge that Mandy was my mate. What I hadn't considered was how much she'd come to mean to me in such a short time. I was entranced by her, in love with her, and committed to spending the rest of my life with her. It was the reason for the special treat. They were a means of enticing her and seducing her before I informed her that she was my mate and asked her to be mine forever.

When she'd stopped by my cabin this morning, we'd agreed to meet for lunch. Time seemed to drag, and I couldn't wait any longer. I was a couple of hours early and didn't care. Being away from Mandy was agony. I needed her like I needed my next breath, to know she truly accepted me as her mate.

MANDY

The two days after the dinner with Nick's family had passed without incident. The few times I'd talked to Reese, he made sure to let me know they hadn't heard anything from Bishop and there hadn't been any more break-ins.

The only thing that had changed since that night was my relationship with Nick. He was more attentive, more protective, and made sure we spent every afternoon together.

I was working on the last cabin slated for repairs, which meant the project Reese had hired me for was nearly complete. My father would be coming back to work soon, and I'd have more free time to resume my classes. It also meant I wouldn't have a daily reason to be spending time at the resort.

The idea of not seeing Nick every day had me dragging my feet to collect my toolbox off the bathroom floor and head to the kitchen. I'd fallen in love with him, and I still had no idea if he was planning to stay or if I should hope for a future together.

We'd planned to meet for lunch, and, if I could work up the nerve, I was going to ask him about the direction of our relationship. If he wasn't going to be around, I needed to be prepared, to protect my heart from the impending hurt I knew was inevitable.

I opened the cabinet underneath the sink and surveyed the pipes. Everything would need to be replaced. I'd learned that Carl and Dale, the two guys who'd harassed Nick and me at the ice cream shop, were the ones responsible for tearing things apart before Bryson had interrupted them. Luckily, the shelf was still okay. There were a few water stains, but no signs of permanent damage.

The sound of gravel crunching on the drive outside drew my attention. Noon was a few hours off, but it wouldn't be the first time Nick had shown up early. I rushed to the door and peered through the screen. My smile faltered, and I froze with my hand on the door handle. Dale and Carl were getting out of a fancy red truck.

They had a lot of audacity to show up here again, and in broad daylight. It took me a second to realize they'd parked next to my truck and knew I was here. Dread inched along my spine. Somehow, I didn't believe they were here to finish the job they'd started.

These were big guys, and wrench or no wrench, I didn't stand a chance against them. A locked door wasn't going to prevent them from getting inside, but it didn't keep me from closing it anyway and flipping the dead bolt. Bryson had stopped by about a half hour ago on his rounds, and I had no idea when he'd be back.

I slipped the cell phone out of my pocket and swiped Nick's number. After two attempts and nothing, I checked the screen and saw that I only had one bar. Damn the spotty reception. Frustrated, I shoved the phone back in my pocket.

Pounding on the door made me jump. "Hey, pretty thing. Let us in. We just want to talk." I recognized Dale's voice and knew better than to believe anything he had to say.

"Yeah, right," I muttered to myself and headed for the bedroom at the rear of the house, a plan formulating along the way.

"We know you're in there, so you might as well open the door."

Once I reached the room, I rushed around the bed to the window on the opposite side. I pulled on the string to draw the blinds upward and covered my mouth to stifle a cough from all the dust I'd shaken loose.

Please, please, please open. I flipped the lock securing the two panes of glass, then reached for the handle on the lower frame. The darned thing creaked but didn't budge.

"Open the fucking door," Dale hollered, banging on the wooden surface even harder, reminding me that I was running out of time.

I reached for the wooden strip on the upper portion of the frame and shoved with everything I had. The old wood scraped inside the tracks, the window jamming to a stop after moving a foot. It was going to be a tight squeeze, and I'd probably end up scraped and bruised. Left with no alternatives, I slid one leg through the opening. I had my chest pressed against the window ledge when I heard wood splintering, followed by a loud crash.

"Where the hell is she?" Dale snarled.

"She has to be here somewhere," Carl said. "You look around up here, and I'll check the rooms at the back of the cabin."

My pulse accelerated, the pressure in my chest

tightening. I drew my other leg over the sill and leaned, letting gravity do its job. I'd miscalculated the drop, lost my footing, and hit the ground, landing hard on my ass. I slapped a hand over my mouth to muffle my groan. After scrambling to my feet, I rubbed my bruised backside. I didn't have time to close the window and didn't bother. It wouldn't be long before Carl reached the bedroom and realized where I'd gone.

Staying low, I pressed against the wooden exterior and crept toward the back corner of the building. My odds of escaping were slim. If I could get to my truck, I might have a chance of getting away from them, because going into the woods wasn't an option. They were wolves and could easily track me if I ran. I shuddered, trying not to imagine what they'd do to me if they decided to shift.

NICK

I strained to control my anger when I reached the driveway in front of the cabin and spotted the large red truck parked next to Mandy's work vehicle. I recognized it immediately as the same truck I'd seen Carl and Dale driving the night they'd harassed us at the ice cream shop.

What the hell were they doing here, and, more importantly, where was Mandy? If they'd hurt her in any way, they were going to die. I jammed my foot on the brake pedal, skidding to a stop, Bear and the container of brownies ending up on the floor. I shoved open the door, slamming it behind me to keep the dog inside. I'd barely made it past the hood when Mandy came barreling around the corner of the cabin, headed for her truck.

"Nick!" she yelled, switching directions and heading straight toward me. Though she appeared unharmed, I smelled her fear. The scent invaded my nostrils and increased my wolf's agitation. She threw herself into my arms. "We need to leave." She forced the words out between pants.

The screen door burst open, and Dale rushed outside, jumping off the porch at the same time Carl rounded the corner, chasing after Mandy.

"Look who decided to show up." Dale rolled his shoulders and took a step forward. "The boss has plans for the girl, so you might want to get back in your truck and leave before it gets ugly." He growled and flicked his hands, extending his claws.

"Nick." Mandy clutched my arm tightly, her face paling.

"She's not going anywhere." I pushed her behind me, positioning myself between her and the two males. I mirrored Dale's actions, allowing a partial shift.

"The boss said I couldn't kill anyone, but he didn't say anything about causing some pain." Dale's sneer exposed an elongated set of canines.

"Mandy, I want you to take my truck and go to the lodge. Find Reese and Berkley." The keys were still in the ignition, making it easier for her to get out of here.

With the threat to our mate, my animal's rage was insistent, pushing me closer to a complete transformation. In my wolf's frenzied state, there was a chance I'd lose control, that I'd turn feral. Mandy could get hurt, and I wanted her as far away from here as possible.

"No, I won't leave you." She pressed her hand to my back, her voice filled with anguish.

"Please do as I ask. I have to fight, and I can't focus if I'm worried about your safety."

"Nobody has to get hurt," Carl said and gave Dale a brief nod. He sidestepped to my left, widening the gap between them, no doubt trying to get to Mandy.

"Go now," I ordered and lunged at Dale, the closer of the two threats. I caught him around the waist and took him to the ground. He shoved me aside and swiped at my chest, his sharp claws ripping through my shirt and cutting into flesh. I winced and rolled, distancing myself from his next attack. It was hard to ignore the metallic odor of blood filling my nostrils or the pain searing across my skin. The wounds weren't deep and would heal quickly, but it didn't mean I wouldn't suffer until they did.

During the scuffle, I'd lost track of Carl and quickly glanced around to see if I could locate him. He was nowhere to be seen, but Mandy had reached the driver's side of my truck. Bear had his small paws pressed against the window and was barking furiously. Trapping the dog inside had saved his life. If he'd gotten out, he would have gone after the males and ended up dead.

I focused my attention on Dale and the easiest way to incapacitate him. Being a target for other shifters, the cocky, more arrogant ones who thought they had something to prove, was one of the downsides to being a wild wolf. No matter where I went, I'd eventually end up in a fight. Luckily, I learned quickly and knew being the aggressor was the best and fastest way to win in most situations.

I launched myself at Dale again before he had a chance to get off the ground. As I'd hoped, the move was unexpected and caught him off guard. I doubled my fist and landed a hard punch to Dale's jaw, rendering him unconscious. With our accelerated healing abilities, he wouldn't be down long. Hopefully, it would be long enough for me to find and incapacitate Carl. I sprang to my feet, noting that my truck hadn't moved and Mandy wasn't in it.

I frantically glanced around and found Carl with his hand over her mouth and an arm wrapped around her waist, pinning her arms to her sides. He was dragging her backward and stopped when he reached the passenger door of his truck.

"Let her go." I took a few steps forward, giving Carl a vehement glare. The man was dead and didn't know it.

Carl lowered his hand from Mandy's mouth to grip her neck. As soon as he released her waist, she grabbed his arm, trying to wrench free.

"Stop," Carl growled and tightened his grip on her throat.

Mandy gasped, and I froze. If he applied enough pressure, Carl could easily snap her neck. With his other hand, Carl reached behind him and opened the truck door. Instead of shoving her inside as I'd expected, he pulled out a gun and aimed it at my chest.

Dale groaned, waking sooner than I'd thought he would. He rubbed his jaw and rose from the ground, his movements slow and jerky. His gaze landed on me, and he snarled, "You're going to pay for that."

"Dale, forget about him and get your ass over here," Carl ordered.

"What?" Dale snapped, then grinned when he saw that Carl had Mandy. "Well, this changes things." He shuffled to the truck.

"Take her." Carl shoved Mandy at Dale, his aim at me never wavering.

"Mandy." I inched forward, uncertain whether I could survive a gunshot wound and not caring. I wasn't going to let them get her into the truck. My wolf was like a caged animal beating against the bars to get free. The transformation was coming whether I wanted it to or not.

"Nick, don't," Mandy pleaded, a tear trickling down her cheek.

The next few seconds seemed to move in slow motion. Carl squeezed the trigger, and I felt a painful prick of pressure in the flesh below my shoulder. When I glanced down, I'd expected to see blood from a bullet wound, not the small silver dart with the feathered orange end sticking out of my chest.

"No," Mandy screamed and struggled against Dale's grasp.

I tore the dart from my chest and tossed it aside. Staggering forward, I tried to reach Mandy. I was too late to stop the drug eagerly working its way through my system. My legs weakened, and I dropped to the ground, landing on my hands and knees. I crumpled on my side, Mandy's beautiful face blurring before my eyes. I'd never felt more helpless in my life. They were going to take her, and there was nothing I could do to stop them.

"Don't worry, pretty thing, your boyfriend will be fine. He'll just have one hell of a headache when he wakes up." Dale's contemptuous voice was the last thing I heard before darkness claimed me.

CHAPTER FOURTEEN

MANDY

I was wedged between Carl and Dale on the front seat of their truck and felt like a child squished between two hulking males. They hadn't been forthcoming on why they'd taken me. I knew I should be worried about what they were going to do with me, but I was more angry than afraid. All I could think about was Nick, the forlorn expression on his face before he'd ended up unconscious in the dirt. I'd feared the worst when Carl had pulled out the gun and aimed it at his chest. Nick was alive, and that was all I cared about.

They hadn't tied me up, blindfolded me, or tried to keep their destination a secret when they headed into the mountainous area near Hanford. Did it mean I was expendable, that my life would be over whenever they got what they wanted?

Dale draped his arm across the seat behind my head and shifted his weight so his thigh brushed against mine. "Relax, sweetheart. No one's going to hurt you." With his other hand, he tugged on a tendril of my hair.

"I'm not your sweetheart, and don't touch me." I

smacked his hand away and inched closer to Carl. Of course, there wasn't much room to move, so the small space I'd put between Dale and me meant I was now pressed against Carl.

Dale laughed. "Feisty. I like it."

Carl squinted and shot him a warning glare. "Leave her alone."

"What? I'm just having a little fun."

"Well, don't. The boss is going to be pissed when he finds out I had to tranq her mate. What do you think he'll do if he finds out you couldn't keep your hands off her?"

They thought I was Nick's mate. I tensed and sucked in air. Surely Carl was mistaken. If I was really that important, wouldn't Nick have said something to me? Unless he was planning to leave or, worse, was disappointed he was stuck with a human for his mate.

He'd been so attentive and caring lately that I didn't want to believe it was possible. I swallowed past the large lump forming in my throat, unwilling to accept that I somehow wasn't what he'd expected, wasn't what he wanted.

"You worry too much," Dale grumbled, then turned his head to stare out the window. Carl's words must have carried some weight, because Dale silently brooded and left me alone for the remainder of the trip.

It wasn't long before the back road Carl had taken from the cabin connected with the main two-lane highway leading to the Hanford Regency. *Please let it be our destination.* The employees would no doubt be loyal to Bishop, but that didn't mean he could control the guests. I wasn't above making a scene, and with plenty of witnesses, Carl and Dale wouldn't be able to keep me from escaping. That little nugget of hope was quickly extinguished when we drove about a half mile past the hotel's entrance and Carl entered a private access road.

I was taken aback when we rounded a curve and slowed to a stop near a thin wooden structure resembling a guard shack. A man casually dressed in a black shirt and pants stepped out and waved us through. I was curious to know what other kinds of business dealings Bishop was involved in that required him to be this cautious about his safety. No wonder my father had warned me to stay clear of the man.

At the end of the drive was a massive two-story home with a luxurious natural landscape. The alterations to the property seemed fairly new. The house was vaguely familiar, and it dawned on me that I'd been here years ago with my father to do some plumbing work for Leo Turner, the previous owner. I'd heard he'd retired somewhere down south to live near his daughter and her family. I didn't know Desmond Bishop had been the one who'd purchased the property. A fact I had confirmed shortly after Carl ushered me into an office and insisted I sit in a plush chair opposite an oversized mahogany desk.

For a man who had no problem breaking the law, Desmond certainly had good taste. The room was decorated in shades of green and accented with hints of mauve and gold. It was a design the interior decorator in me could appreciate.

I startled at the sound of a man clearing his throat. I'd been so busy taking in the nuances of the room that I hadn't heard him enter. Glancing over my shoulder, I wasn't surprised to see the owner of the house dressed to the same degree with which he'd decorated his home. His chocolate-brown hair was cropped close to his head, not a strand was out of place. The amber rimming his dark eyes added to the intensity in his already unnerving gaze.

"I'm Desmond Bishop. Welcome to my estate."

Though I'd never personally met the man before today, I'd recognized him immediately. I'd seen his picture in the newspaper when they'd published an article announcing the hotel's opening. The man exuded a haughty charm, and even if I wasn't seeing it for myself, I'd heard enough distasteful things from my father and his friends to know he couldn't be trusted and was extremely dangerous.

"It's Mandy, isn't it?" He politely held out his hand, then returned it to his side when I refused to take it.

Even though he maintained a forced smile, the muscles of his jaw tightened. This was a man who was used to getting his way and didn't appreciate being snubbed. Too bad. I didn't think being kidnapped qualified for the use of good manners.

"Being forcefully manhandled isn't exactly the same as being invited, now is it?" Seething, I raised my chin and dug my nails into the lush fabric on the chair's armrests. I wasn't about to show him any fear. It was a wasted effort since he was a wolf and could scent any changes in my emotions.

"I do apologize for the methods my men used in bringing you here." He cast a disapproving glance at Carl and Dale, who were quietly standing near the entrance. "I'd hoped our meeting would have happened under better circumstances. I can assure you I have no intention of causing you any harm."

I was having a hard time believing his statement and held back a snort. I already knew Desmond would do whatever was necessary to get what he wanted. Or rather he'd have others do it for him. The man's suit was too immaculate, his manicured fingernails too clean, and the skin on his hands too soft to be someone who did any real labor himself.

"Why am I here?" Memories of what Carl had done to Nick flashed through my mind. They'd expected trouble. Otherwise, they wouldn't have shown up with a dart gun. I had some theories, but I wanted to hear Desmond's explanation.

"Let's just say you're an insurance policy of sorts." He propped himself on the edge of his desk, stretching out his long legs and crossing them at the ankle.

"For what?"

"To ensure I have Nick and his family's cooperation.

Once they sign the deed to the resort over to me, you'll be free to go."

"I could go to the police, file a complaint, and have you arrested."

He released an impertinent sigh and twisted his lips into a confident smirk. "But you won't. It would be your word against mine. And since there isn't a scratch on you, who do you think they'll believe? A lowly plumber or a reputable businessman?"

I hated that he was right. I might have grown up here, but I wasn't anyone special, didn't have any of the power he possessed. With a sheriff and two deputies, Ashbury didn't exactly have much of a police force. "One of your guys injured Nick, and the other one shot him." I tossed a thumb in Carl and Dale's direction. "Is that going to be their word against his too?"

"I'm afraid you misunderstand the severity of the situation." He unhooked his ankles and got to his feet.

His eloquent way of speaking was getting on my nerves, and I wished he'd get to the point. "Then explain it to me."

"It would be a shame if Nick had an accident." He twisted the silver band inlaid with numerous diamonds on his right pinky finger. "The woods around here can be deadly. Who knows what might happen to a wolf when he goes out for a run?"

Desmond's insinuation was clear, Nick would end up dead if I didn't agree to his terms and keep my mouth shut. Dale's snicker, along with the echo of knuckles cracking, reinforced the threat. I would do anything to protect Nick, to keep him alive. Overwhelmed by defeat, I slumped my shoulders and sank into the chair.

NICK

"Nick, wake up." My mind slowly crept from the

135

darkness and was greeted by a pulsing ache stretching across my forehead. Something jostled my shoulder, and I felt the repeated application of a slick, wet surface attacking my cheek and chin. I forced my eyes open and focused my blurry vision on Bryson's hulking frame. "Had me worried there for a minute." His deep frown lessened, and he snatched Bear and his slobbering tongue away from my face.

"Where's Mandy?" I croaked through my dry throat, then glanced around before my mind registered that she was gone.

"She's not here."

"They took her." I tried to sit up, then wished I hadn't when another sharp jab spliced my skull.

"Take it slow. It looks like they shot you with enough tranquilizer to take down an elephant." Bryson gripped my forearm and helped me to my feet. "It was the same guys from before, wasn't it?" He tipped his head toward the road leading away from the cabin. "I recognized the scent and saw the same tire tracks."

"Yeah." I slowly nodded my head. "Bishop's men."

"Come on, I'll take you back to the lodge."

I staggered a few steps. "I need to go after her." I braced my hands against the hood of his jeep, waiting for the nausea pummeling my stomach to ease.

"No can do." Bryson tapped the handheld radio attached to his belt. "I already contacted Reese, and he'll have my ass if I let you go after her in this condition." He opened the passenger door to his jeep.

I was ready to tear into him when he shoved me into the seat. In his bear form, he'd be a worthy opponent and could kick my ass on a good day. High metabolism or not, with the remnants of whatever drug Carl had shot me with still coursing through my system, I didn't stand a chance.

"Think about this logically. If Bishop wanted her dead, they wouldn't have taken her. Something else is going on, and if you go after her by yourself, you could end up getting both of you killed. Better to talk to your brother, figure out our next move, and work as a team."

I stifled a snarl, hating to admit that Bryson was right. After setting Bear in my lap, he got into the vehicle and drove us back to the lodge. It was a short drive, yet it seemed to last forever. My anxiety and the need to find Mandy was compounded by my wolf's increasingly hard-to-control determination.

Once we arrived, Bryson reached for Bear and tucked him inside one of his massive arms. "I'll take care of the dog. You go talk to Reese." He tipped his chin in the direction of the main entrance, where Reese and Berkley were rushing outside.

"Thanks." I slid out of the jeep and headed toward them. The throb in my head was down to a dull ache, and I was glad my reflexes were finally cooperating.

In seconds, my siblings were at my side. "Oh my God, Nick. Are you okay? All Bryson said was that you'd been shot." Tears filled Berkley's eyes.

"I'm fine…really." I gripped her hand, trying to comfort her. "It was only a dart filled with some kind of tranquilizer."

"Who did this?" She didn't wait for me to answer before running her fingertips over the tears in my shirt. She reached for the hem, lifting the fabric and examining the partially healed wounds.

"One of Bishop's guys." I glanced at Reese. "They took Mandy."

"Fuck." Reese shoved his hand roughly through his hair. "Let's go inside, and you can fill us in on what happened." He straightened his shoulders. Determination bounded from every step Reese took as he led us into his office. Once inside, he promptly aimed me toward the chair opposite his desk.

I was too keyed up, and the last thing I wanted to do was sit. However, I was still struggling from the aftereffects of the drug and reluctantly complied with my brother's wishes. Reese walked around his desk and dropped into his chair, and Berkley made herself comfortable on the arm of my chair. I spent the next few minutes filling them in on my encounter with Carl and Dale.

"It sounds like Mandy was their intended target," Reese said.

"Yes...to get to me." I rubbed the back of my neck, the pain in my head dulled in comparison to the pressure constricting my chest. I'd failed to protect my mate and could lose the one person who meant everything to me.

"I need to get out there and find her." I started to get out of the chair, and Berkley gripped my shoulder, urging me to stay seated.

"And we will," Reese said. "I know you care about her. We all do."

I pinched the bridge of my nose, striving for calm. "You don't understand."

"What don't I understand?"

"She's my mate." I hadn't wanted to tell them until I'd spoken to Mandy first. I needed them to know, to realize why I was so close to losing control.

"I knew it. You were acting way too possessive and protective around her." Berkley seemed satisfied with herself. She tapped her chin, her smile fading and her gaze narrowing. "Wait a minute. Mandy doesn't know, does she?" She punched me in my sore shoulder, and I winced. "Why didn't you tell her?"

"Berkley, not now," Reese ordered.

"Fine," she snapped, giving me one of her looks that said we would be finishing this conversation later. "If I was able to figure it out, then there's a good chance Bishop did too."

Reese and Berkley didn't have to say anything for me to know what they were thinking. Bishop had chosen Mandy because of her connection to me. He knew if he had her, he had me. Wolves, specifically wild ones, would do anything to protect their mates.

There was a knock on the door, and Bryson stuck his head inside. "Bear's done doing his business. Mind if we join you?"

"Not at all." Reese waved for him to enter.

Bear took a few cautious steps inside, sniffed the floor and the air. Satisfied by what he smelled, he rushed over to me and began whining and pawing my leg. "It's okay, boy." I picked him up and set him on my lap. Stroking my hand along the dog's back helped soothe some of my anxiety. Too bad it didn't have the same effect on my wolf.

"In case you were wondering, the tracks from the truck were headed in the same direction they took that night after the break-in." Bryson propped himself on the edge of the lateral cabinet.

"Is it possible they took her to the hotel?" Berkley asked, picking Bear up off my lap and cuddling him against her chest.

"No, he's too smart for that. It's too public and the first place anyone would look." Reese pulled out a drawer of his desk and retrieved a business card. "I think it's time to give Bishop a call." No sooner had he placed the card on the desk than the phone began to ring.

"That's probably the slimy bastard now," Berkley said.

"Let's find out." Reese picked up the receiver. "Yes, Nina." He listened to whatever she was saying, then nodded. "Put Mr. Bishop through." He glanced from Berkley to me before pressing the speaker button.

"Good afternoon, Reese. I assume you've spoken to Nick and know why I'm calling." Desmond spoke as if Mandy's kidnapping was an everyday business transaction.

"What do you want, Desmond?" Reese didn't waste any time getting straight to the point.

I fisted my hands in my lap, the tips of my emerging claws digging into my palms and drawing blood. I had plenty of things I wanted to say to the asshole. I knew it would be better to let Reese handle things, because threatening to rip Bishop's balls off wasn't going to get Mandy back.

"You already know the answer. It's what I've always wanted."

"The resort." Reese spat the words through gritted teeth.

"Yes." Desmond's smug enthusiasm grated on my nerves. "You sign the deed over to me, and I will release Nick's mate."

"How do we know she hasn't been harmed?" Reese asked.

"You have my word."

"Not good enough," I growled, scooting forward to perch on the end of my seat.

Reese held up his hand to silence me. "I'm afraid we're going to need some proof."

"Very well." Desmond sighed. "Carl, go get Ms. Jenson."

A few minutes later, I could hear Mandy yelling in the background. "Let go of me. I can walk by myself." I could only assume it was Carl who'd made the mistake of touching my mate again. Added to what I owed him for the dart, and I was determined to make our next encounter painful for him.

"Other than confirming your good health…" Menace resounded in Bishop's tone. "You will not tell them anything else." The man was doing his best to ensure we didn't find out where he was keeping her.

"Nick, are you there?" Mandy asked.

"It's me. Did they hurt you?"

"No. Other than being a little manhandled, I'm fine." Hearing anger in her voice was better than hearing fear. I needed her to stay strong.

"Don't worry, we'll get you back safely," Reese diplomatically interjected.

"I know you will." There was a pause, then Mandy spoke again. "Hey, Desmond."

"Yes."

"Nice house. Did you kidnap one of old man Turner's family members to convince him to sell it to you?"

"That's enough," Desmond roared, cutting her off. "Carl, get her out of here."

Mandy was an intelligent woman and was trying to tell us where she'd been taken. I didn't know what property she was talking about, but she'd confirmed our suspicions that Bishop wasn't holding her hostage at the hotel. Reese and Berkley had spent a lot of time here. It was possible they knew what Mandy was talking about.

"Nick, no matter what, don't give him what he wants," Mandy shouted before a door slammed. From the irritation I'd heard in her voice, I imagined sparks of anger darkening her crystal-blue eyes. Her bravery filled me with pride and fear at the same time. Taunting Bishop was a bad idea and could get her killed.

"As you heard, Ms. Jenson is fine. I'll give you until sunrise to bring the papers to my hotel. After that, well…I can't make any promises regarding her health." Desmond disconnected the call, his stipulated threat clear.

I'd been in more fights than I cared to remember, and not once had I ever taken a life. That status was going to change quickly if Bishop or any of his men laid a hand on Mandy.

"Reese, you're not seriously thinking about turning the resort over to that scumbag, are you?" Berkley stroked Bear's fur, a flush of pink brightening her throat and cheeks.

"No, but until we figure out how to get Mandy away from him safely, we need to make him believe we're playing along."

"What about Mandy's reference to this Turner person? Does it mean anything to you?" I asked.

"No, but Roy might know. He's lived here all his life and done work for quite a few people." Berkley pursed her lips. "We need to tell him about Mandy."

"I'll take care of it since I'm the one who didn't keep her safe." Failing to keep my promise to her father added another layer to the guilt already weighing down on me.

"Nick, this isn't your fault. This is on Bishop, and we'll take care of him." Reese opened a side drawer and pulled out a worn leather-bound book with the word "directory" stenciled on the front. "Let me make some calls."

"To who, the cops?" As a rule, shifters didn't involve law enforcement in their problems.

"I know it's hard, but I need you to promise me you won't do anything stupid. We'll figure this out...come up with a plan to get her back," Reese said.

Stupid would be letting the men who took Mandy live after I found them. I pushed out of the chair, intent on leaving, but Bryson stepped in front of me and blocked my path. "I'd be feeling the same way if it were my mate. Reese is right. We need to make a plan, handle this correctly, and stop Bishop once and for all."

I gritted my teeth, then crossed my arms and turned to face my brother. "I'm listening."

"James had friends, people who might be willing to help. We'll start with them."

CHAPTER FIFTEEN

NICK

Even though our deadline to meet Bishop's terms wasn't until the following morning, we were running out of time. Each passing minute heightened my anxiety and gnawed at the tenuous grip I had on my wolf. It had been harder than hell to wait for Reese to organize Mandy's rescue. I'd lost my temper and come close to releasing my animal more than once.

It was two hours after sunset, and I'd spent the last ten minutes nervously pacing the ridge where the small group Reese had gathered stared through the darkness at the lights illuminating Bishop's property below. Four vehicles, two SUVs, Reese's truck, and Bryson's jeep were parked haphazardly behind us on the grated gravel surface of a roadside overlook.

Berkley had been correct when she'd said Roy might know about Turner. He'd been able to give us the exact location of the property.

Add in the information Reese received from some of his retired military contacts and we had the name of the dummy corporation and the alias Bishop had used to purchase the house and the surrounding ten acres of land. Land he'd turned into a protective compound of sorts, supporting my theory that the man had gained a few enemies over the years. If we'd had more time, I was certain Reese's friends could have gotten us blueprints and layouts of the entire area.

Besides myself, my siblings, and Bryson, there were six others in our rescue party. Roy, of course, had insisted on being present. He was the only human, and with his foot encased in the cumbersome boot, he wouldn't be able to come with us. I was certain he'd blamed me for his daughter's kidnapping and was surprised when he pulled me into a fatherly hug and assured me of the contrary.

The other five males, old friends of James's, had volunteered without being asked and were more than willing to help us do whatever was necessary to get Mandy and apprehend Bishop. I couldn't remember their names but was thankful for their help and made a mental note to find a way to repay them later.

"Bishop is prepared for intruders." Reese lowered his binoculars. Since shifters had great night vision, he didn't need special goggles to see in the dark. "It looks like he's got one man guarding the access road, three watching the front perimeter of the building, and four positioned at various spots along the back of the property." My brother's time in the service showed in the way he'd organized and was leading the rescue.

"Is everyone clear on the plan?" Reese's gaze touched each person in the group. After receiving simultaneous nods, he turned his attention to our sister. "Good. Berkley will stay here with Roy."

"Like hell," she huffed. "You're not leaving me behind."

I wasn't worried about Reese. He could take care of himself. Blood would be spilled tonight, and I couldn't live with myself if any of it belonged to Berkley. "I have to agree with Reese. This is going to be dangerous, and you could get hurt."

"Oh no, you don't," Berkley snarled, slapping her hands on her hips and leveling a glare at both of us. "Mandy is my friend, so you don't get to play the overprotective big brothers."

"Berkley, could you listen to me just this once?" Reese pleaded, holding out his hands and trying to console her.

"No." She avoided his reach. "I'm going, and you can't stop me."

Bryson normally didn't get involved in a conversation unless he had something important to say. "Excuse me." His rumble vibrated around us. "Are we going to stand here all night and argue, or are we going to take down this asshole?" Once he had everyone's attention, he continued. "Berkley can run with me."

"Awesome." She smiled at the bear shifter as if he was her new best friend.

Reese pinched the bridge of his nose. "Fine, she's officially your responsibility, but if anything happens to her, you'll have to deal with Nick and me, understood?"

Bryson grunted and gave him a sharp nod.

Reese turned to Berkley, his furrowed brows more defined. "And you." He tweaked her chin. "No heroics and follow Bryson's lead."

"Will do, sir." She winked and gave him a mock salute.

Reese reached for the hem of his shirt. "Everyone else, strip and shift."

Finally. My pants barely touched the ground before my wolf had taken over.

MANDY

I hated being used as a pawn, a way to force the people I cared about to give up their home. Trying to escape was pointless. I was dealing with wolves, natural-born hunters, and I had a feeling Desmond wouldn't hesitate to order his men to hunt me down and do their worst.

He'd worked in his office, and other than the courteous escorts to the restroom by Carl, he ignored me. I'd spent most of the afternoon confined to a chair and under the watchful scrutiny of Carl and Dale. My anxiety had reached intolerable levels, and my limbs had started to complain.

Though the men who occasionally entered the house to speak with Desmond openly leered at me, undressed me with their gazes, and added to my nervousness, he'd kept his word and hadn't let anyone touch me—so far. I'd overheard him tell Reese what my fate would be if they didn't provide the deed to the resort by morning. I didn't trust Desmond to keep his word, and since threatening him with the police hadn't seemed to bother him, I'd bet anything my life would be over come morning.

I clung to the belief that Reese would figure out the clue I'd given him about the property's previous owner. Hopefully, Berkley would contact my father and get the details they needed to find me before the deadline tomorrow.

The warning I'd given Nick hadn't earned me any favors with Desmond. He'd been irate, and I was surprised he hadn't retaliated. A status that could change any second if I wasn't careful.

After receiving a call, Desmond rose from his desk. "Please, come with me." He waited for me to stand, then led me down a hall and into an elegant dining room. "Contrary to what you might think of me, I'm a good host." Centered in the middle of the room was a long, rectangular table that easily sat fourteen people. He waved his hand toward one end, where numerous platters of food had been placed along with two place settings.

Dale and Carl had followed behind us and remained standing in the hallway outside the open doorway. It appeared that Desmond was too good to dine with the help.

He pulled out a chair and motioned for me to take a seat, then proceeded to occupy the adjacent chair placed at the head of the table. The food looked delicious, and the aroma from the thinly sliced beef, pink in the middle, filled the air and teased my senses.

"I appreciate the hospitality, but I'm not hungry." My stomach rumbled, confirming my lie.

Desmond quirked a disbelieving brow. Ignoring my comment, he lifted one of the platters and offered me the first helping.

"No, thank you." I shook my head and clasped my hands together in my lap. Since they'd drugged Nick, there was no way I trusted Desmond not to try the same with me. It would be a lot easier to get rid of me if I didn't put up a fight.

He released a displeased sigh and draped a cloth napkin across his lap. "I have no intention of poisoning you, if that's what you're thinking." He placed several slices of meat on his own plate.

Poison had been an afterthought, and my contemplation of its use dissipated with the sound of heavy, booted feet pounding against the hall's ceramic tile.

"I need to speak with the boss."

I glanced toward the doorway where one of Desmond's men hovered next to Carl.

"What is it, Jonas?" Desmond asked, waving a hand for the man to enter.

"Sir, I'm sorry to bother you." The man glanced from me to Desmond and didn't appear too happy about the news he was bearing. "There's a man at the gate claiming to be Mr. Turner's nephew and demanding to see him."

As far as I knew, none of Turner's relatives lived in the area, so who the heck was the guy at the gate? Desmond shot a malevolent glare in my direction, then pushed out of his chair and angrily tossed his napkin onto the table. As soon as his back was turned, I grabbed the knife from my place setting and slid it into the bib of my overalls. It wasn't much of a weapon, but it was better than nothing, and I prayed he'd been too distracted with whatever was happening at the gate to notice it was missing.

"The man refused to leave even after he was informed that his uncle no longer lived here. I was told he smelled like a cat." Jonas slid his hand through his hair. "Wasn't the previous owner a human?"

"It's a distraction," Desmond shouted, then released a growl so loud, it echoed through the room and pulsed against my eardrums. His chest heaved, and claws emerged from his fingertips. I stayed seated, too afraid to draw attention to myself. Even Jonas, who was several inches taller and bulkier than Desmond, lowered his head and nervously took a step backward.

Carl and Dale cringed slightly but didn't move. Apparently, they were used to their boss's outbursts.

"Contact the gate and alert the rest of the men to be ready for an attack from the rear of the property," Desmond ordered.

"Yes, sir." Jonas practically fell over himself trying to get out of the room.

Desmond shook his shoulders and flexed his fingers until the claws disappeared. When he turned to face me, his demeanor was controlled and calm. "Too bad your mate and his family didn't take my offer." He glanced toward the doorway. "Carl."

"Yes, sir." Carl took an obedient step forward.

"You and Dale take Ms. Jenson upstairs and put her in the guest room. I'll deal with her personally once things have been handled."

I assumed by "handled," he meant permanently taking care of whoever he thought was coming for me. I slowly got to my feet, bracing a hand on the table to steady the tremor rippling through me.

"Let's go." Carl walked around the table, gripped my arm, and dragged me from the room.

The muscles in my legs refused to work properly,

making our ascent on the staircase a struggle. Dale followed closely behind us. He made some appreciative noises, and I knew he had his lustful gaze focused on my backside.

I'd never been so glad to be shoved into a bedroom alone and have a door slammed in my face. I'd been battling shock and fear for so long, I wasn't sure how I'd made it to the bed before collapsing into a heap on the edge.

If Desmond's assumptions were correct, and I had no doubt they were, Nick, Berkley, and Reese were trying to rescue me, and it could mean death for all of us. Knowing they were wolves—strong, proud, deadly—didn't stop me from worrying about them.

I glanced at the slim crack below the door, noting the occasional moving shadow. It was wishful thinking on my part not to expect Desmond to keep a guard posted in the hallway. Curious to see what was happening outside the house, I walked to the window and peeled back the curtains. The evening sky in the distance was clear, filled with hundreds of stars. The area behind the building was easily visible, lit up by the numerous lights on the building's exterior and enhanced by the glow from the three-quarter moon.

Needing to dispel my apprehension and get some fresh air at the same time, I slid the window open and took a deep breath. I was too far off the ground to jump, and judging by the number of men I saw moving around below, Desmond was more than prepared for any kind of trouble.

After staring at the tree line for who knows how long, I spotted movement slipping in and out of the shadowed areas between the trees. At first, I thought my vision was playing tricks on me, that my current stressful state had caused me to imagine it. Long seconds passed before I saw more movement and squinted to get a better look. There was something out there. Something low to the ground and definitely not human.

"What are you doing?" I heard Dale's voice and jumped. He stepped into the room, shutting the door behind him.

I turned and eyed him suspiciously. "I could ask you the same thing."

"I believe you owe me an apology."

"For what?" If anything, I was the one owed an apology for the way I'd been treated today.

"I haven't forgotten about your cute little trick the other night at the ice cream shop." He took an imposing step toward me. "Better yet, forget the apology. I'd rather have a kiss."

I wasn't going to let that happen and inched my hand along my side and within reach of the knife hidden inside my bib. "Where's Carl?" I glanced over his shoulder, silently wishing for the other man to miraculously come through the door. I wasn't fond of either male, but since Carl had protected me from Dale earlier, I felt somewhat safer with him.

"He got called outside, so it's up to me to protect you."

I wasn't reassured by his statement. If anything, I was exceedingly wary.

"If someone as fine as you were my mate, I would have claimed you already." He moved another step closer. "I'll bet I can make you forget that worthless wild wolf."

"I'm not interested, so please leave." I moved away from the window, quickly glancing around the room for a way to escape. With the door on the other side of the room, he had me boxed into a corner between the bed and the wall. The only way to get around him was to go over the bed.

When he reached for me, I pulled out the knife, thrust it into his chest, and dived onto the mattress.

"You bitch," he bellowed.

The knife sailed across the room, bounced off the wall, and clattered on the wooden floor. I'd nearly reached the other side when he latched on to my ankles and dragged me backward. I screamed and gripped the edge of the bed, pulling the silken comforter along with me.

Dale fisted the braid at my nape and yanked me to my feet. He encircled my waist, his thick-muscled arm tight and constricting. "If you'd cooperated, I could have made this pleasurable for both of us." His hot, rancid breath grazed the skin on my neck. "Now, I'm going to take what I want."

Bile churned in my stomach, and I gasped for air. My struggles were useless. He was going to rape me, and there was nothing I could do to stop him.

Dale undid one clasp on my bib and was reaching for the other when the wood around the door handle splintered and the panel banged against the wall. A huge black wolf, shoulders hunched and fangs bared, stood in the doorway.

Nick.

His silvery-gray eyes glowed with a feral intensity—menacing and lethal. He stalked into the room, releasing a growl so low and guttural that even I shivered.

NICK

I'd almost been too late. The thought continually filtered through my mind.

After everyone had shifted, we'd spread out to approach the front of Bishop's property from different vantage points. When one of his men tore from the house with a warning on his lips, I knew Reese's friend, Preston Harker, had arrived at the gate and was causing problems for the guard. As we'd hoped, most of the men were headed to the expanse of forest behind the house, leaving the front unprotected.

While the rest of the group engaged Bishop's men, it was my job to get inside and retrieve Mandy. If I encountered Bishop, even better.

I'd been relieved when I caught a glimpse of her in the second-story window. The momentary feeling of gladness was short-lived with Dale's appearance, closely followed by her scream.

My plans to break a window to enter the house changed when I discovered someone's oversight had left the front door standing partially open. Creeping through the house, I was surprised to find it empty. Not even Bishop was lurking around. As much as I wanted to be the one to immobilize him permanently, getting to Mandy was my main concern. No interference meant I'd get to her more quickly. The few seconds it took me to rush upstairs and follow her scent to the bedroom seemed to take forever.

By the time I was crashing through the door, my wolf had gone feral and taken over completely. I was a silent passenger, able to think and speak to my wolf but unable to control the anger ripping through him. Rage was a mild way of explaining the raw emotions tearing through me when I found Dale trying to remove Mandy's clothes. My animal would do whatever was necessary to protect her, and for once, I wasn't going to stop him.

Dale scowled and shoved Mandy aside. "I've been looking forward to this."

Not nearly as much as I was. The bastard had dared to touch my mate, had planned to hurt her, and for that, he would die.

And die painfully.

I waited until Mandy had safely backed into the corner before focusing on Dale and releasing a challenging snarl.

Dale tugged his shirt over his head. "Once I'm finished with you, I'm going to help myself to your mate."

Even though Mandy didn't seem surprised when Dale informed her of her importance to me, I still wanted to tear out his throat in the worst way. Either she was suffering from shock, or she already knew she was my mate.

Her safety and keeping her as far away from Dale as possible were my primary concerns. I leapt the short distance between us, not giving him a chance to finish undressing. I hit him in the chest and hurled us toward the partially opened window. The back of his shoulders slammed into the upper pane, shattering the glass and littering the ground beneath us as we tumbled out the window. The two-story drop wouldn't kill us, but the impact was going to hurt like hell.

At the last minute, I dug my claws into Dale's chest, leaving sharp gashes and shoving away from him. I landed in an upright position, skidding through the rock and dirt, scraping some of the fur off my underbelly.

Dale wasn't as lucky. His back thumped the ground hard enough for me to hear the air whoosh from his lungs. He rolled onto his hands and knees, wheezing and groaning. By the time I'd righted myself, he'd shifted and was shaking off the last remnants of his shredded clothing.

His fur was a light golden brown, and, though he was larger than a normal wolf, his animal was nowhere near the size of mine. I'd learned never to underestimate size. Being smaller didn't necessarily lessen the extent of an opponent's abilities. I carefully circled Dale, studying him for weaknesses, readying myself to attack.

Shortly after we landed, I'd surveyed my surroundings and noticed the rest of my group had engaged Bishop's guards. A couple of the guards had taken off, and of the few who'd remained, two were lying on the ground unmoving. The rest of Bishop's men had shifted and were battling with my family. Two of my late grandfather's friends appeared to be injured badly but continued to fight. Blood streaked the fur on Reese's gray wolf. By the ferocious way he tore into one of the males, I doubted much of it belonged to my brother.

I spotted Bryson across the yard to my left. He was incredibly large for a bear and towered over any wolf here, including mine. True to his word, he'd kept Berkley close and made sure she didn't get into any trouble. She fought as fiercely as my brother when Bryson gave her a chance to enter the fray he had going with two of the other male wolves. I could tell her wolf was pissed, and had a feeling poor Bryson would be hearing about it later when they were all back in human form.

Seeing Mandy appear in the doorway of the house's rear entrance reminded me of what Dale had planned to do to her. I wanted the male dead and for this to end quickly. I needed to hold her in my arms and reassure myself that she hadn't been harmed by the other male's actions.

Dale's wolf must have noticed her too, because he didn't waste any time going for my neck. I jumped to the side at the last second, and his teeth grazed my shoulder. Pain skittered across my skin, the metallic scent of blood filling my nostrils. I spun as he passed, latching on to his flank and sinking my teeth into his flesh.

His yelps and attempts to shake free only incited me more. I clamped down tighter, tasting his blood and increasing the damage to his injury. Dale's wolf curled sideways, snapping and snarling, getting close to my face. I had no interest in losing an eye and was forced to let him go.

I parried, bit, and clawed at Dale, meeting each of his attacks with one of my own until exhaustion settled into my muscles. By now, the remainder of Bishop's men had been subdued and some had shifted out of their animal forms. Berkley's wolf was standing protectively next to Mandy, while Reese and Bryson, still maintaining their animals, had taken positions on the opposite side of Dale's wolf. They understood our fight was personal and wouldn't interfere unless Dale decided to forfeit the fight and make a run for it.

Dale was limping and losing a lot of blood from the wound on his flank. I wasn't without honor and shook my head at him, a silent warning not to continue, giving him one last chance to walk away and live. If he was smart, he'd shift and concede the fight.

The cocky bastard didn't understand the significance of being smart and lunged at me again. This time, I held my ground and absorbed the brunt of his attack. He realized his mistake too late when I clamped my jaws around his throat. No amount of struggling was going to win his release. After several hard shakes of my head, the bone in his neck snapped, and he went limp.

It was a shallow victory, one filled with remorse, and I howled my disgust when Dale's wolf dropped to the ground. Satisfied that our mate was no longer in danger, calm settled over my wolf, and he relinquished control back to me and my human form.

"Nick." I heard Mandy's worried voice and turned seconds before she flung herself into my arms.

CHAPTER SIXTEEN

MANDY

Kidnapping, death threats, and nearly being raped had left me exhausted and emotionally drained. I was thankful to be alive and glad that the people I cared about most hadn't been seriously injured. Shortly after we arrived at the lodge, those who'd participated in the fight used some of the guest bathrooms to clean up.

Other than leaving long enough to take a shower and change into some of Reese's clothes, Nick had been overly protective and hadn't left my side.

Berkley had grabbed some bags of chips and prepared sandwiches, then had everyone settle into the large gathering room near the lobby. Besides her and Nick, Reese, his friend Preston, and my father were the only ones who'd returned to the lodge.

I'd only been able to thank three of the five men who'd been friends to James Reynolds for helping with the rescue before they'd returned to their homes. The other two men had sustained some serious injuries during the fight, and Bryson had taken them to the hospital in Hanford.

"Are you sure you're okay?" My father studied me with

his concerned gaze. It had been the third time he'd asked me the same question in the last few hours. He was sitting nearby in a tan, cushioned chair with his booted foot propped on the matching ottoman.

"Dad, I'm fine." I swatted Nick's hand when he snatched another chip from the plate sitting on my lap. Bear was curled up on the long sofa on my other side, his head on his front paws. Every so often, he'd groan and open an eye, hoping I'd toss him a morsel. "No begging." I smiled and scratched him behind the ears.

Conversation around the room had slowly ebbed. Without saying a word, Berkley picked up the empty platters and headed in the direction of the kitchen.

I speculatively watched my friend leave, then whispered, "Nick."

"Hmm." He had one arm draped across the couch behind my head and was absently stroking the skin on my shoulder.

I glanced at Reese's friend from the military who was comfortably perched on the expansive stone hearth near the fireplace. Preston hadn't spoken more than a few words and was quietly sipping beer from a glass bottle. Every time his emerald gaze found Berkley, which seemed to be consistently, amusement tugged on the corners of his lips. Berkley, on the other hand, was doing her best to ignore him.

"Is Preston a cat?" It was the only thing I could think of to explain my friend's behavior.

Nick's hand froze. He narrowed his gaze, glancing at Preston, then back at me. "Yes, why?"

He had finally calmed down, and I didn't want to cause him any more stress. "Just curious." I leaned closer and placed a soft kiss on his cheek.

"Roy." Berkley returned to the room and offered him a key card. "It's getting late. Why don't you stay here for the night, and someone can take you home in the morning?"

He took the card. "If you're sure it's not a problem."

"Not at all. Come on, I'll show you to your room." She waited for him to lower his leg, then helped him out of the chair.

"It's safer if we all stay at the lodge tonight." Berkley stopped next to Nick and handed him a card as well.

"Thanks." Nick took the key, surprising me by not arguing that he needed his space and wanted to stay in his cabin.

"Good night, sweetheart." My father hovered behind me and pressed a kiss to the top of my head. "I assume you'll make sure my daughter gets settled." He directed the statement at Nick.

"I'll take good care of her." Nick squeezed my shoulder.

I always felt safe when I was with him, and his reassuring words settled around me like a warm blanket.

"You do that." My dad hobbled after Berkley toward the elevators on the opposite side of the lobby.

"Pres, why don't you come with me?" Reese stood and angled his head to the rear of the lodge. "I'll give you a tour of the private quarters and show you where you'll be staying."

During introductions, I'd learned that Reese had hired Preston to be his new head of security. With all the trouble they'd had with Desmond, combined with his mysterious disappearance, having additional protection around the place sounded like a good idea to me.

Now that Nick and I were alone, I remembered that he still hadn't said anything about me being his mate, and I was suddenly nervous. He'd risked his life to save mine, and I knew he cared about me, but it didn't lessen my trepidation at wondering why he'd kept it a secret. I had a lot of questions and didn't know where to start. "Nick, we need to talk."

"I know." He removed the plate from my lap and set it on the coffee table. Instead of getting comfortable as I'd expected, Nick got to his feet, taking my hand and pulling me along with him. The next thing I knew, my feet left the floor, I was cradled in his arms, and a squeal had escaped my lips.

"Bear, let's go." He grinned and snuggled me closer, then headed toward the stairs leading to the second level, with the dog following behind us.

I tightened my grip on his neck. "I thought we were going to talk."

"We are." His long strides took us to the door at the end of the hall. He adjusted his grip, then scanned the card Berkley had given him and entered the room.

After setting me on the end of the king-size bed, Nick grabbed a pillow and placed it next to the wall on the floor. "Sorry, boy. You'll have to sleep here tonight." He patted the cushion and waited for Bear to settle in the middle of it.

"He usually sleeps on the end of the bed," Nick offered by way of an explanation. "I have plans"—he sat next to me, desire filling his gaze—"and I don't want him getting in the way."

"Plans?" Heat pooled between my legs, my nipples hardened, and I bit my lower lip.

Nick ran the pad of his thumb along my jaw. "First, we talk."

NICK

It was hard to stay focused with Mandy sitting this close to me. When she'd said we needed to talk, I knew she'd want to know why I hadn't told her about our connection. I swallowed the nervous knot constricting my throat and took her hands in mine. "Mandy, you're my mate."

"How long have you known?" She didn't pull away, and she sounded curious, not angry.

I took it as a good sign and continued, "From the

moment we met." It was the truth. I might have argued with my wolf and denied it in the beginning, but deep down, I'd known.

"Oh." Her shoulders slumped, and she lowered her head. "Was the reason you didn't tell me because you're disappointed that I'm human, or that you were planning to leave at the end of the year?"

"Neither." I hated that my own insecurities had caused her to doubt her self-worth. I grasped her chin, forcing her attention back to me. "You're perfect...better than I deserve. I was on my way to tell you this morning. I didn't get the chance..."

"Because Carl and Dale showed up."

I nodded. "Yeah...they kind of ruined my plans."

"So, why didn't you tell me sooner?"

"At first, I didn't want to say anything because of what I am."

She shook her head. "I don't understand. You know being a shifter doesn't matter to me."

"Wild wolves are loners for a reason. They have short tempers, can lose control, and sometimes go feral."

"You mean like earlier tonight?"

"Exactly."

She placed her hand on my cheek. "I love you and your wolf. I know neither of you would ever hurt me."

"You do?" It took a few seconds for me to comprehend what she'd said. "Wait, you love me?"

She nodded. "I was a goner the minute you asked me out for ice cream."

I tugged her onto my lap so she straddled my thighs. "I love you too." I gently brushed my lips across hers.

"Are you aware that wolves mate forever?"

"Yes," she whispered.

"If you agree to let me claim you, I'll never let you go."

She slid her hands along my shoulders. "And if I agreed, what would a claiming involve?"

"A lot of pleasure and a bite to mark you, right about

here…" I touched the skin where her shoulder met her neck, my cock growing hard at the prospect of making her mine permanently. "So everyone would know you're my mate."

MANDY

Hearing Nick tell me he wanted to claim me, to make what we had permanent, made my skin tingle with anticipation. His erection pressed against my core, creating an achy need that only he could quench. "Will it hurt?"

"According to what I've heard, there's a brief amount of pain followed by intense pleasure."

"That doesn't sound too bad…the pleasure part, I mean." I smiled and wiggled against him.

He groaned and gripped my hips. "Does this mean you're consenting to my claim?"

"Yes," I murmured and reached for the edge of his shirt, then tossed it on the floor after he helped me pull it over his head. I knew he'd been injured in his fight with Dale, but he'd refused to let me examine any of his injuries afterward. "Oh, Nick." I gently skimmed my fingers over the pink and partially healed marks on his chest. Some of them were no doubt remnants from when he'd landed after going through the window. I'd been so afraid I'd find him on the ground dead when I'd rushed to stare through the broken glass.

"It's fine. They'll be gone in no time." He grasped my hand and placed a kiss on my palm. "Let me make you mine."

I nodded and slid from his lap, unhooking the clips on my bib, then making quick work of removing the rest of my clothes. Nick stood and did the same, encircling my naked body with his arms. I ran my fingers along his chest, placing kisses on his skin and flicking his nipple with my tongue.

He groaned, gripping my nape and angling my head for a kiss. A kiss meant to possess and be tender at the same time. I moaned, leaning into him and stroking any part of his skin I could reach.

Nick spun me around to face the bed, then pulled my back against his chest. He kissed and nibbled my shoulder, slowly working his way to my neck. He cupped my breast and gently pinched my nipple, a taunting torment that tugged at my core. I gasped, needing something to hang on to, and settled my hands on his hips.

He moved his hand along my abdomen, dropping lower and sliding his hand between my legs. He slipped two fingers inside me at the same time he grazed the spot where he said he was going to mark me. The orgasm was immediate, unexpected, and left me trembling. He continued moving his fingers, drawing out my pleasure until I thought I was going to collapse in a heap on the floor.

I barely had a chance to recover before I found myself in the center of the bed on my hands and knees. Nick knelt behind me, nudging my legs wider. I glanced over my shoulder, noting the feral flicker in his eyes, a reminder that his wolf wanted to be part of the claiming. He pushed aside my braid, then gripped my hips and slid inside me. His movements were anything but teasing and slow. Each powerful stroke was designed for optimal pleasure and quickly shoved me toward another climax. He kept one hand on my hip to anchor me in place and used the other to tap my clit in time with his thrusts.

"Mine." The animalistic growl was the only warning I got before he sank his fangs into the soft flesh covering my shoulder.

I experienced pain, pleasure, and another orgasm at the same time. All I could do was grip the comforter and let the overwhelming sensations wash over me.

Seconds later, Nick had his arm wrapped around my waist, groaning through his own release. He rolled onto his side, taking me along with him. When the tremors finally subsided, I realized he was lapping the skin around my bite.

"I might have gotten a little carried away," he said, sounding a tiny bit guilty. "Does it hurt?"

I moved my shoulder, then rolled onto my back so I was facing him. "It's not that bad. How does it look?"

He presented me with an annoyingly arrogant grin and kissed my cheek. "Like I marked my mate."

CHAPTER SEVENTEEN

NICK

It had been three weeks since Bishop's disappearance. No one in the shifter world, at least according to Reese's contacts, had been able to find any traces of him. It was as if he'd vanished from the planet. I could only hope.

If Bishop ever decided to make an appearance again, we were ready for him. With Preston's expertise, he didn't have any problems taking over and was doing a great job as head of our security.

This morning marked a new beginning, and I was having a hard time containing my excitement. I drove my truck about a quarter mile from the lodge before parking it on the side of the road.

Mandy sat in the passenger seat, patiently clutching Bear. "Can I take this off now?" She fingered the edge of the fabric covering her eyes. She couldn't see where I'd taken her because I'd insisted on blindfolding her before we left my cabin. Or I should say *our* cabin since she'd been living there with me since the night I'd claimed her.

"Don't move. I'll come around and get you. And no peeking," I warned, slamming the door and rushing to her side of the vehicle.

I lifted Bear off her lap and set him on the ground, then turned to unsnap her belt and lift her off the seat. "I've got you." I carefully set her on her feet, then placed my hand on her lower back and guided her forward. I led her to the edge of a large clearing. From this distance, I could see bits of the lodge through the trees. After a few more steps, I stopped and untied the material. "Okay, now you can look."

She squinted, giving her eyes time to adjust to the bright sunlight.

"What do you think?" I asked.

"It's beautiful..." She appeared confused. "Can you give me a hint on what I'm supposed to be looking for?"

"This is our new home." The cabin was fine for now, but once the resort was fully functional, Reese and Berkley had agreed to let me build a larger home for Mandy.

She wrinkled her nose. "Are we being kicked out of the cabin? If we are, I can ask my dad if he'll let us stay with him until we find another place."

"Nobody is kicking us anywhere." I took her hands. "This is where I plan to build our new house."

"What? I..." She glanced at the area again as if seeing it through different eyes.

"Damn, I should have given you this first." I fished a tiny black box out of my pocket. "As far as I'm concerned, you are my mate and we'll always be together, but I wanted to make it official in your world." I dropped down on one knee and popped the box open to display a golden band intricately carved with Celtic knots. Two wolves faced each other on either side of a brilliant topaz.

Mandy stared at the ring and hitched her breath.

"I wanted a stone that matched the blue in your eyes, but if you don't like it, I..."

A tear trickled down her cheek. "It's perfect." She swiped at her face, then held out her hand so I could slip the ring on her finger. "And the answer is yes."

"The answer?" I didn't remember asking a question. Then I realized what she was talking about and said, "Oh." I got to my feet and wrapped my arms around her waist. "Mandy Jenson, will you marry me?"

"Yes, yes, absolutely yes." She threw her arms around my neck and gave me a passionate kiss.

"And now that Barb has agreed to be Roy's new apprentice, there's no reason you can't go back to school and get your decorating degree. We can even build you an office in our new house if you want to start your own business."

"Really? You'd do that for me?"

"Mandy, I love you. I'd do anything for you."

She nipped my chin. "Does that include going back to the cabin and having some fun?"

"Of course." I hoisted her over my shoulder, enjoying her giggles as I strolled back to the truck and set her inside.

She was my mate, my love, my future. Most of all, with Mandy, I finally had a place I wanted to call home. She'd been a temptation I couldn't resist, and now that I had her, I was never letting her go.

ABOUT THE AUTHOR

Rayna Tyler is an author of paranormal and sci-fi romance. She loves writing about strong sexy heroes and the sassy heroines who turn their lives upside down. Whether it's in outer space or in a supernatural world here on Earth, there's always a story filled with adventure.

Printed in Great Britain
by Amazon

78636657R00098